MW01518313

Spt 28/2022

PILGRIM

a novel by

BRAD THOMAS BATTEN

FOR CUZ D,

To the JOURNEY.

Peace + oranges

B.

 FriesenPress

One Printers Way
Altona, MB R0G 0B0
Canada

www.friesenpress.com

Copyright © 2022 Brad Thomas Batten
First Edition — 2022

All rights reserved.

No part of this publication may be reproduced in any form, or by any means, electronic or mechanical, including photocopying, recording, or any information browsing, storage, or retrieval system, without permission in writing from FriesenPress.

Cover photo and author photo courtesy of Annet Zuidhof.

ISBN
978-1-03-914804-8 (Hardcover)
978-1-03-914803-1 (Paperback)
978-1-03-914805-5 (eBook)

1. FICTION, LITERARY

Distributed to the trade by The Ingram Book Company

Given the times (quarantine, lockdown, shutdown, shut in) I've taken my novel *JourneyMind* (2001) and processed it through the winemaker's press once again. I asked, How would I write about love and loss, the tragic and the beautiful, now? The container is similar; the contents have been renewed, altered, expanded upon, evolved. Call it a reboot, an updated map, a whole new fruit. Call it *Pilgrim: A Novel.* Enjoy.

"God is at home,
it's we who have gone out for a walk."

Meister Eckhart (1260–1329)

I TERRA INCOGNITA

AVENUE ROAD

A few months ago, Father and I were sitting at the kitchen table in his studio. We were studying old world maps and spinning his desktop globe, tracing pilgrim routes and voyages of exploration, when Father said, "I imagine all true journeys of the heart begin where the dead have left off, or have failed in their attempts to liberate."

I never knew the power of a word over the body. Not until Father's words seized us, scouring mouths and limbs. The elegant terror of death searing us to the bone. So that there would be nothing left but wind, ash, and the low, blue whisper of an unwalked road.

There are those who lose their lives and are unearthed again after years of wandering, heads down, fingers fixed like divining rods. Others descend into their lives because the fear of God has them on hands and knees, wrestling with belief. I'm on the descent because, like Lazarus in his four days of tomb darkness and death-wrap, I was somewhere inside the hold of disfigured metals, swallowed up whole. The night grinding through the rear-view mirror, the smashed windshield, the slow rap of sleet and gasoline along my arm. What was it that slipped in behind my eyes, scraping retinas, skullcap, brain stem. Shadow-events cascading through my mind, my body pausing in remembrance of itself.

Hogtown. Old Muddy York. Toronto the Good. Where the pull of black ice conceals itself under a December moon. It's 1988 and zero degrees Celsius. The degree of our undoing. I look up through the underbelly of the city. Toronto. A grid city for the most part, eight or nine diagonal streets, marked with a few dips and curves and dark rivers. It's a city with a Great Lake as its original host, the glacial basin out of which its quick, fertile lands first emerged.

The rivers Humber and Don, once teeming with fish life, now struggle the narrow course. Roads, highways, train lines, and bridges extend over river valley systems, rearranging the influence of things that flow. Precambrian layers groan beneath housing developments: backyards, banks, churches.

The ravines pull the city in closer to its lap and pulse. Potent underworld ecosystems, half-travelled footpaths, swollen root systems that bleed up through an escarpment that defines the city's latitudinal thrust. Emerging through the ravines, through angled trunks of oak and maple, willow and elm, where houses lean with looking glass windows and streets spin out from the ends of branches, all modern roads must angle up and down the city's escarpment; sloping climbs that, when walked, challenge the heart and lungs. When driven, the climbs and descents are an unfelt silence of something forgotten.

Avenue Road harnesses one of the steepest intrusions over the escarpment. A quick northern rise, or a southbound descent, with a dip and a rise before Dupont, then another dip and slow rise toward Davenport. On hard, rainy days, or when a sudden snowfall and thaw hit, water, grey and cold, fills the dip between Dupont and Davenport. Sewage systems struggle to keep up with the onslaught of water. When the temperature drops again and the freeze returns, it's like an ice rink there. Black ice, almost transparent, magical. Branches and electrical wires along the road become coated with ice, shining droplets suspended in mid-fall, like frozen bells.

I saw the truck coming, headlights streaming in the rearview mirror. We were stuck in a dip, traffic backed up, black ice, and a green light. The back tires spun, grinding; the smell of burning rubber coming through. I looked for a way out, begged the car, then froze at the wheel. Elle must have heard the truck approaching, skidding, sliding. Her ears a strange, finely tuned string instrument. She looked at me. Those gracious, flashing orbs, so green.

She said, "Have faith." Meaning, try again, put your foot to the gas, gently now, and navigate us out of here, be a good captain and honour the winter sea. Her voice was not demanding, had little fear.

Then Father's hands appeared from the back seat, grasping Elle at the shoulders, a gesture reassuring and strong. Those same hands that set up an easel and canvas and showed me what lives behind a world of paint. Hands with eyes in the palms. Those hands that, when I was a child, placed a bath towel over my wet head and rubbed and rubbed until my hair was matted dry, squeaky clean. The world beneath the towel dark, silent, and safe.

For a moment the light inside the car surrounded us, a series of constellations contracting and expanding, then settling within the St. Christopher medal which hung from the rear-view mirror. Who is the patron saint of stillness? Because everything stopped, collapsed like the contrasting hues in one of Father's still lifes, the one depicting an orange set against the base of a white pine. Such allurement there, it made the eyes ache to look again.

Then the headlights in the rear-view mirror erupted, flooding the insides of the car, flooding my muscles, my lungs; turning strength to snow. World upside down.

There was little left of the car. A gash through the passenger side, the St. Christopher medal sent through the windshield, spinning away. The stabbing weight of the steering wheel against my chest, glass shards spilling across my face, into my mouth. Whose flesh and blood were those? Father? Elle?

What is it to lose a life and to find a life? The journey-work of a seed falling into blackened earth and dying, but dying to yield a rich harvest. Having to give our lives over to a labour of grace with fecundity and guile.

They pulled my body from the wreck. Pulled my left arm, dangling like a fuse, singed with oil. They had no choice but to lay me down in an ice-slicked pothole at the side of the road and douse the fuse, my arm, skin, coming through the torn sleeve. Someone put a jacket over me, heavy as stone, so that I wouldn't blow away. They covered my face with a sweater, a wool cardigan, buttonholes in place of my eyes.

I could feel the heat of my breath become smoke. Like a burnt offering, a first-born son.

A circling blue glare slashed the night, broke through the buttonholes through which I kept an eye on the passing world. *Die with eyes wide open*, I thought, to become a faithful witness to the world of *is*. Above my head bare branches leaned, stutter-tongued. The cold air pulled at the ground beneath my spine, suckled at the exiled pothole. Snow was laced with grit and the remains of a gaseous impact of a truck and Father's small, two-door vehicle slammed up against the residual shock of two other vehicles and a third from behind. Metals folding, cringing under the weight of the frozen air. Deformed plastics, broken glass, hinges, and springs splintered along the roadside, biting into black ice. My throat choked on a cold blue scream, and everything stopped again.

What is it to die while in between worlds, to be taken down into the mysterious ground of those who have gone before us? The earth like a dark lover easing open her limbs. What is it to lose everything of the heart that distinguishes us from the night?

I caught a glimpse of something crawling. Two figures, loose rind, hardly human, clasped as one. Till death do us part. But there was no parting, not yet. My lover, Elle, and my father, joined, at one in their groping crawl, moving now through a hole in the side of what was once the shape of a car. Two bodies, soul-animals with newly formed appendages, moving toward me, gasping and bloodied, suddenly transforming, going under ice and the road like eels, electric shadows nearing my body, then quietly entering me, pore by pore, gash by gash, finding some heart space and curling up. Calling my body sacred ground.

I sat up, tried to stand. I couldn't feel my legs, my arms. Someone, a stranger, just a hand, told me to stay still. Wait.

Everything turned red. The taste of gasoline and glass and blood in my mouth, scorched my throat. The night got colder, cracking beneath snow and ice. I felt the underworld at my back opening up, felt its aching jaws.

Okay, I thought, *take me too*.

Atonement is not easy. It is not found or grounded or even released in a scream. It limps, unsure of its footing. It agonizes, grunts, before it can voice its lament. Before it can learn to praise.

It was ten days of recovery, without the celebration of their faces, in a hospital cut off from the wind. Days and nights were spent in and out of consciousness, held in my bed by night sweats and fever-spiked dreams. Shock. Medical tubes, weird-looking instruments slender as snakes, were wound around my body. A fractured ankle, a bruised jaw, bruised ribs and torso, small burns like birthmarks along my left arm, contusions near my spine, and a concussion. Each breath kindled loss. Elle and Father burrowed further in, rooting themselves, tapping my heart for sustenance. And there was that other presence, that estranged one, a third. Mother. Dead fifteen years but now moving a withered hand up through my skin, my hair. The cancer started in her liver, moved to the pancreas, and took her whole body in no time. Doctors closed their notebooks, then their eyes. Father and I sat with her after the heaving, the vomiting, washing her body down, wanting to tell her something fresh. Mother managed a smile, a flicker beneath the eyes, then went into the silence. Violent white. Her slow, sore body told us its story. Mother, the summer stock actress, the stages she graced across the country. And Mother the eternal patient, the institutions she had come from and gone to, the heavy depressions, the medications, the side effects, the sudden unfolding and leap. Mother the dancer with the cigarette going.

We watched her wither, her moist, wide cheeks caving, curling under; gone. The world moved aside as if to accept one more body, one more life and death to mark the planet . . . Mother Was Here. She was unconscious her last forty-eight hours, still with morphine. Then, a minute or so before 3 a.m., she just opened her eyes.

In the hospital bed she snuggled up inside me, some-where near my spleen, weaving blood, dirges, whispers. Reunited with Father, twined like tall grass, anchored near the base of my spine.

Elle—Danielle—exchanged glances with Mother for the first time.

They pulled my body from a wreck, drunk with the after-taste of red, raw glass chewed into sand, into blood, and back. My hands sometimes reach out, tremble, as if to grip a phantom steering wheel. My right foot alternates between brake and gas pedal, loss and the permission to survive. I roll over, the bed a torn page.

I slip through visions, earth's wailing walls. I see my shocked animal-spirit angling along a dark, unmapped road. No traffic, no lights, nothing over my shoulder but a lone grey wolf, bucking the threat of extinction. I prowl roadsides, log sorts, bent, abandoned farms, hardwood forests, trees replete with the sound of songbirds: warbler, hermit thrush, purple finch. Branches and leaves drip like nightfall over gnarled, half-sunken pathways that meander slowly, break off then narrow into a far horizon where earth and sky collapse into a single, blackened fold. I cannot say if I'm fading here, the core in decay, or if there's something else trembling again, in orbit, a gesture of what is to be.

401 WEST

Time stumbles, puts on a black cloak.

I journeyed west, leaving what burned, leaving the quiet Ontario snows, flakes glancing off my boots. A packsack, jeans, a few shirts, a sweater, a change of socks and underwear, a small army surplus bag, a sleeping bag, the jacket on my back, and a leather medicine pouch containing Father's ashes.

I rode a bus from Toronto to a hassle at the Windsor-Detroit border. I possessed a one-way ticket only into the States. US customs wanted to know how I intended to make my way around their country and back out, and how much money did I have? ("I'm just travelling. Trying to walk off something. Something that happened. I'm not a threat to national security.") They refused me entry and pointed me back across the border bridge. I waited in a coffee shop, pondered the road and bridge, eyes still. A customer, a Franciscan priest, therapist and sociologist, a man named Father Brian responded to my pondering, my story, and offered me a lift. He was on his way back to Chicago. He'd handle customs and get me into the Land of the Free without my being questioned. A slight man, angles of flint in the eyes, sweet wine on the breath, Father Brian put me up for a few nights in his small parish in South Chicago. He had one of the largest book collections I've ever seen, a stream of titles and manuscripts from kitchen to bedroom to laundry room and back. St. Augustine through Aquinas, the desert Mothers and Fathers to the Rhineland Mystics, Meister Eckhart to Merton to Zen; Jung, Frankl, and beyond. But Father Brian was about to give it all away. "At sixty", he said, "it's time a person divests themselves of their possessions and begin to travel light." So a book auction was to be held and the proceeds would go to the parish and its many other needs.

"There are two kinds of knowledge," he was saying, a bottle of wine between us. "There is that of description, and that of acquaintance. There are all kinds of specialists writing on politics, psychology, religion, environmental stress, and the new world order. I get it. Not trying is not an option. That's what mature, healthy spirituality is all about, facing our suffering head-on. Think Jesus, think the Buddha. And like Impressionist life studies there is only one way to see and move through that suffering and that is to be immersed in the stuff of life and all its glory and terror, even in the radiant decline of a sunflower. For that, you have to go to the crossroads of your life, right into the ditches and alleys; you have to walk."

So Father Brian had me out in the streets, on foot, a whole day. South Chicago. I saw the soiled faces, deserted public squares, sidewalks gaping with cracks. I saw dead pigeons, rats, gutted newspapers, and tenement houses;

forgotten freedom cries, potholes widening, pushed aside by deindustrialization and demolished social programs, as if the civil rights movement never quite reached the north, got derailed somewhere around the Mason-Dixon Line. I saw in the face of a young man the strain of masturbation one second, a heart attack the next. Ecstasy was everywhere being converted into a drug. The pursuit of happiness plucked clean before its time.

Seeing me off at the bus station, Father Brian added, "Remember, first there is the journey *to* God. Then there is the journey *in* God."

I bused it from Chicago to East St. Louis, then hitched my way to New Mexico in the back of a pickup truck. I left in the dead of night, wrapped in my sleeping bag, the sun tipping into view somewhere over Missouri and scorching my sleep. A warm meal here and there, through Kansas, Colorado, down into New Mexico, downtown Albuquerque. Maybe it was a day's journey, maybe two days. I crashed in a fleabag motel and slept two or three days with the TV going and the stealth of pornographic films whispering from other rooms down the hall. I poured through the Gideon Bible, got hooked on words like burden, light, yoke, easy. I longed for these words to give sustenance to what my body had left behind. I was stubborn for a fresh, shining sound. The language of metals, spittle, and flint. A teaching my parched tongue could soak in.

After a day of stretches and push-ups and sit-ups and burritos and coffee, I rented a beat-up Ford and took to the road. I don't know how long I drove the state behind that wheel. Albuquerque to Santa Fe and back, then east up into the barren hills, through broken-down, diminished mining towns, then south to Las Cruces, circling back through Truth or Consequences, up and down Highway 25 like a displaced dervish, the road my sanctuary. I'd catnap when I felt the need, curl up in the back seat of the Ford or pitch my sleeping bag to the side of the road beneath a lean-to of scrub brush and branches, loosened soils. I had a Thermos full of coffee, a bag of day-old bagels, salami, and cheese. I could drive eight, nine, ten hours without a break. One day I just pulled over, stopped the car, found some hot springs up in the hills, and bathed myself, surrounded by tall pines, until I was red as a tomato and stoned on the heat. Then I ditched the Ford back in Albuquerque, got myself a pup tent, warm gear and supplies, and took to my feet. I walked to Santa Fe, knew the road by heart. I walked another couple of days to the eerie settlement of Los Alamos, home to the bomb, where refugee scientists, Oppenheimer's men, turned the world of spirit and matter inside out. I hooked up with a group of people who made a yearly pilgrimage from somewhere north of Santa Fe to Los Alamos and carried with them soils that were said to be holy. Everyone had their pockets lined with the holy soils, their angelic radiance. And I thought, *Here I am . . . I'm carrying Father's ashes, Father the pacifist who seldom travelled beyond the borders of his beloved Ontario.* Father, who'd spin the globe on his desk like Charlie Chaplin in *The Great Dictator*, close his eyes, and slowly lower his index finger until it rested on the globe, to stop the spin. Wherever the finger would land—the States, the South Pacific, the Old World in its rusted gleam—Father spoke of travelling to that place, of tapping into its sap, but never found the time or unpacked the risk.

Is it the Fates? God's Will? Or the energy of a Universe? Which of these conceives the paths that undo you, the roads nearing those unexpected fault lines where the world plunges freely? Or is it simply the heart that better understands where it is you must go and what it is you must offer once you arrive?

As my companions of the road fed the atomic ground of Los Alamos with the holy soils from their pockets, I gave a thimbleful of Father's ashes, a first sprinkling toward redemption, raw bone meal over the red, red earth.

It was then that the wind began to assemble from the southwest. I did not know its name.

I hitched a ride and then walked a few days toward Chaco Canyon and found my body facing the ancient ruins of the Anasazi, one of those tribes or peoples who simply disappeared or wandered off, assimilated or were annihilated, became dust or the stars, and bore another path.

Four days alone in the ruins, sliding in with the prehistoric soils, the bloodline of stones and cliffs and dry riverbeds. I sat with sunrises and sunsets and star-storms. Eating only dry bread, dry fruit and nuts, tuna from a can. Drinking water and reused coffee grinds reheated over an open fire. I slept under the naked night, nestled in the caves and crevices of the open-roofed ruins, next to the wide, dry river. I woke to the sound of coyotes and the wind, the long, murmuring mornings like an old song. I tapped into the tight drums of the earth, the clashing instruments of weather. I felt my insides kick while the skies closed in and the clouds opened up and the rains poured down for the first time in days, months . . . like her laughter when the sheets are pulled back.

Early morning. Just after six. Coffee by the open fire. The sun over the canyon. A low, flat light. I lift my eye over the coffee mug, straining for balance. I've come here because there is something in the wind that is medicinal, without judgement.

The way she lay in my arms, and the fragile curve of her waist.

Elle. What brought us together? A wild, conspiring design. Your body was like a choir. Jesus, the humming going on inside your belly. It kept me up nights, stunned, in awe. Your breasts taut and slow, firm as dark, anxious seed beneath a black, trembling soil. And that silence inside of you, a core laid bare. So silent I thought at times you had passed away. I suppose even the choir has to sleep.

I saw you first at a dinner party, one of those downtown warehouse situations, overcrowded, music jolting, but you stood out, a sunflower in a roomful of Henry Moore sculptures. You sat at a long table, in behind wine glasses and bottles and vases of lilac, behind bread baskets and salad bowls teeming with greens and reds; you sat over your bowl of pasta (red sauce red wine) with such concentration, the perfect balance between spirit world and animal world. It seemed you gave thanks with every slither of pasta. I remembered something I had read about the poet Rilke, his manner of eating as if making love. I moved closer, inching in, a game of musical chairs; only sitting when the music stopped.

"Someone told me you paint," you said. "Is it true?"

"No, my father is the artist," I said. "I've tried but my thoughts just get in the way."

"Have you read Van Gogh's letters to his brother?" you asked.

"It's on my list."

"What are you reading now?"

"The Great Gatsby."

"The tragic situation of a man and a light separated by miles of water," you said.

"All I see is about three feet between us," I said.

You didn't laugh. Thank God. You sat up, aligned.

"What are you reading these days?" I asked.

"Cohen," you said. *"The Favourite Game."*

I did laugh, sensing an uncertain turn. My body was ignorant of strange directions, of geography and medieval maps worked out by lovers and astrologers. The burned desire of stars.

Slowly now, you whispered, close to me. Slowly taking me in.

When we first made love in your St. Clair attic apartment brilliant with twilight, the window a little frame on the world outside, the walls dotted with poster prints of bicycles and philosophers and folk stars, Van Gogh's *Wheatfield with Crows*, I noticed the crucifix over the bed, the one thing anchored in all that motion.

Like this canyon now, its low, shuddering earth.

You felt my hesitation, turned me over, hands on my chest, through my hair; tender. I forgot my name, my history; Mother's dying. Thank God for small, undisturbed moments, the clarity of our sex.

Once, when the moment came, you savoured the seed, kissed me on the lips and exchanged the fluid. The taste of an unnamed sea.

We held one another a little closer, without daring the other to leave. The space between becoming less and less, trusting the small places where we lay. Our bare bodies beneath a single blue sheet. Shrouded, protected. Saved.

You spoke of your body, earth and death as of three inseparable gifts. "When my time comes," you said, "the soils will take pleasure in making peace between the spirit world and my flesh."

At twenty-five I am too raw to think of last wills and testaments, unwilling to question what the earth knows of my body. I resist your lessons. But there you are, seven days my elder, your wisdom taken in through your hands, in the garden on your balcony. You are certain my body will one day understand.

Everything changes.

We read in the dark, our bodies like two loosened sketchbooks, peeled back, studying the wisdom of unnumbered pages. We used tongues fine as horsehair brushes to detect the faint canvas contours, the small Braille shapes, raised paint chips along our skin. We took detours inside the shade of our mouths, traced hieroglyphics, the deep caverns of Neolithic lovers thawing out beneath the warmth of a kiss.

"It's in the areas of being we least understand about ourselves that we support one another," you said. "There is beauty in imperfection."

You seemed to anticipate death like someone studying weather patterns, or like the child with her ear pressed against a railway track, listening for the power of the locomotive, the distant vibration announcing its approach. Death was always before you, just as the saints taught you.

I sat on the edge of the bed, my ear pressed against your chest, listening—always your pulse there, as sure as earth. Your arms taught me. The soul finds completion in the curve of an embrace.

Elle. I looked at trees and branches, all that embracing going on, slipping into the wonder of your skin, its trembling nobility. The oils we lathered ourselves with so that our sex would be an offering, a purification of those places inside the body that the world could not restore. Edges, succinct fault lines, greening at our touch.

Sundays we took to the road, on bicycles or in Father's car, covering every incline and field from the Niagara escarpment to Tobermory. We attended Mass in small towns—Milton, Orangeville, Wiarton—our desire timed with the breaking of bread and the blessing of the wine, blessing and flowing through our limbs, closer to the source of our hold.

On a hill on the Bruce Peninsula, overlooking Georgian Bay, your family farm. A long view of wild water, hillsides, and sloping fields speckled with apple trees, cherry trees, pear trees; just breathing in all that sweetness left our bodies drunk. We made love beneath the heavy buds, then later beneath autumn's appointed dusk. And the winter nights, the sweeping snows, the cold north wind, we camped out in the barn, in an unkempt room up in the rafters. Your father had put in a small wood stove when you and your brothers were children; board games, hide-and-seek, your first cigarettes. The nights we camped out up there, with the fire always going, we sipped herbal teas and tongued warm whiskey from the lip of a bottle, throats made smooth and hot. We slept nearer and nearer the smouldering embers, our down sleeping bags zipped together as one, our bodies heaving then pouring into one another while the stars broke through holes in the rafters, one by one, splayed like seed, spinning through to dawn.

I missed your funeral. I tried to get back to you, tried to walk out of the hospital. I managed to get myself dressed, half disguised in a baseball cap and an orderly's smock. But the nurses caught on to my limping gait, the crutches, my pale look, and the short stumble in the hall.

When I was finally released—the day unclear, disturbed, inverted as if the snows were somehow growing out of the late December earth—I discovered that your parents had already cleared out your attic apartment, removed the poster prints, the low futon, the blue sheet, the crucifix, Van Gogh's *Wheatfield*, and the lamp with the purple scarf slung over the shade. I fell to the floor in that emptiness; crushed.

I went to your grave near Lion's Head, the view you wanted of Georgian Bay, its rough passing waves. Your grave was still fresh, its haunting imprint, a small mound of snow and earth rising like a belly eight months with child. It made so little sense to me that you were in there, buried and naked without me. I wanted to see your face, your eyes, I wanted to taste the insides of your mouth. I wanted to hold you in your death shroud. I thought of a story my mother's father had told me of the Great War, the Battle of the Somme, no man's land caked with bodies, dirt-brown uniforms against a dirt-brown earth, everything sinking, as if the dead were left to bury themselves there. And my grandfather, shell-shocked, he said, nerves lost in the night, was on hands and knees searching through the mud, the bodies, the fingers of the dead, half sinking half clinging to the surface, searching, he said, for his brother, his blood, having to dig, sniff like a bloodhound, until he found a finger, the back of a hand with the familiar birthmark on it, the one shaped like an island, he said. The Toronto Island, his brother used to say.

But there I was, Elle, disregarding history and its lessons, digging for you. My fingers in the cold, dead grass and earth, half-frozen snow and mud slipping through my fingers and up the backs of my hands, curling beneath my sleeves. I stopped. For three or four days I went to your grave, dug for a minute, hit that frostbitten silence, then stopped. My hands were not prepared to accept your gift, your death, a life beyond the horizon line. Sorrow overtook my body, scattered, like a handful of dirt falling upon a coffin lid.

Those graveside vigils brought little reprieve. Beneath my skin there was a hollowed trunk, heart rot, and shards of black ice. Frozen sap waiting for a tongue-flame of sun.

A friend and co-worker at the restaurant, the place I cut vegetables, flipped burgers, paid my way through university, teacher's college, school books, art books, the rent, said, "Stop going to her grave . . . it'll drive you mad."

I couldn't tell him you weren't really gone. You're inside me, I saw you, crawling from the wreck and circling down my throat, my lungs. Like rainwater down a drain.

How these hands once grasped the things now descending.

Father was cremated, reduced, and capped inside a simple urn. I gave my consent from the hospital bed, convinced that the quicker he received his wish, was burned, the quicker would the fire leave my body and rise.

His Severn Street studio space had been paid off for a year. Father was good at taking care of his space, the one place in the world he swore by, where he could set his feet and feel secure and unhurried before a primed piece of canvas.

I placed his ashes on the windowsill in a brass urn, a smudged prism through which the world struggled with its reflection. I sat with Father's ashes and a bottle of rum, a tiny wake accompanied by Miles Davis; *Kind of Blue*, *Bitches Brew*, *Siesta*. Drunk with ashes and the dead; what else? Drunk with memories of Father's voice reading *Treasure Island* to me as a child—"Fifteen men on the dead man's chest, Yo-ho-ho and a bottle of rum!" My first glimpse into the journey of a word, then the world.

I moved slowly through Father's things. Old art magazines; an atlas thrown open on the floor; ripped, tangled, coffee-stained maps of Ontario parks: Temagami, Quetico, Algonquin. Rivers and lakes and bog systems running the landscape like shadowy veins.

Father had two heroes of the brush: Van Gogh and Tom Thomson. Father believed Van Gogh painted simply to touch the sorrow of the Suffering Soul who had lost the threads to his or her God. He loved the spiralling limbs and fields of a Van Gogh landscape, how those same spirals could be found in a person's face. In Thomson, it was all about bringing the wilderness home, Father believed. He loved the mysterious blank spots on a Thomson board that seemed to pick out the whys and wheres of how we journey the world of spirit and matter, naked flashpoints with the ability to undo certainty. Flashpoints knowing a measure of death.

Father marked his own canvases with images of tree trunks, close-ups of thick bark, contrasting interiors of wood and stone, the underside of rind. Father used paint like sap, stuff so fluid, so intoxicating, lifting itself like muscular seed, like trailing sperm into the womb that was canvas. He painted, or crafted, fragrant knots in the sides of dying trees, driftwood wound so tight, so still, that sometimes just one glimpse of Father's works made my spine snap back, as if realigning itself. As if I had been struck by something not seen.

Father was seldom satisfied with any of his works. There was always something missing, something more to do or add or take away, he said. Something he couldn't put his finger on. Like a blind spot blind to another blind spot. He'd binge paint, lock himself in the studio, ply his vision, enter into the driftwood and broken branches and bark peels and pine cones and rocks we had hauled into his studio, waiting for something to emerge. He painted, he said, so that death would forgive him his ignorance. Then he'd just stop, snap, close up the studio windows. He'd leave his sacred space and lock up, leaving behind the call of unfinished works.

He'd then binge on odd jobs; house painting, cabinetry, or he'd buy a rundown house, renovate it, flip it, and bank the money. He entered a world of objects that wouldn't fight back or tear at his hands like the ragged edges of an unfinished canvas. After weeks or months away from the studio, he'd return, a monk clutching some remnant of the world found in a forest, suddenly aware that he belonged to a larger community, a wife, a child, a few chairs, and a tabletop. And he'd paint as if pursuing long, late shadows of the sun going down, until the contrast of light and dark became sharp aches in his joints, so insistent he couldn't paint anymore. A third hand pushed him back, down into his chair. He'd stare at a canvas, or spin the globe of his desktop, a finger held in orbit, waiting, then landing—Asia, the Greek Islands, deeper in the South Pacific.

Mother's death overturned everything, a death that levelled him, a wedge between us. Looking into my face, the crease of my eyelids, the long bright lashes, how my hair swept brown into blond like Mother's, he kept saying he saw her in me, then he would turn away. His own intense Still Life turned against him. Paint waited to be cupped and held. Colour drained from his body as if it had exhausted all probability of light and belief. His works, which contained so much beauty, could also unearth so much tragedy. He could no longer carry on a conversation. Loss hooked him by the mouth. He moved through the studio, threw open the windows, as if it would make a difference, just throwing open a window. All his prayers became dislodged from the acts of his hands.

He looked at my young boy's face, a study in knots, bare features like birch bark stripped back, nerve endings raw with my own black grief. I would have exchanged my life for a cup of water. I didn't know if I was supposed to hold him or if he was supposed to hold me. Was there a protocol for sorrow?

"Look, I'll see you in a few weeks," he said. "I just can't look at you right now."

A few weeks became a few months. The spare sense of his absence. During my thirteenth year I was moved out of our Elm Avenue duplex and off to a grandparent's, a cousin's, an old family friend's, whoever might spare a weekend.

Absence in presence and presence in absence. Which of the two makes us believe in the other first?

Father renounced everything in life that couldn't be proved in paint.

Is that snow? Or distant sands lifting, blowing in, circling, falling feather-like and white.

I look over this sober landscape, canyon walls scorched and baked, and try and tap into its cavities of wounds and healings, its initiatory process. The things that mark us, that things that call us forth. There is an openness and depth and strength here that pulls me in. Have these reddened walls been carved out by grief? Have they reconciled themselves with the shine of both day and night? I just don't know. Most sorrow travels away from the sun. My mind with one sorrow, my body with another. Like Father, I sit back, wait, and spin the globe.

I bundled up Father's paintings and empty canvases, half-finished works, new and used paintbrushes, turpentine, easels, wooden knives and spoons, spatulas caked in multiple pigments, jars, dented lids, cloths and smocks and blue jeans so full of dried, hardened paints, discoloured fingerprints, that the materials stood their own ground, curled up with a kind of integrity, or a longing, like a cat or a dog waiting for its master to return.

For a time death required me to replenish my mind and body in the grace of night and the wind. I found a storage space for Father's works, emptied my own small Annex apartment and filled the storage space with our stuff, paid it off, a five-year plan, no interest. I laid Father's paintings on their sides, like stacking wine bottles or firewood, energy stored away for the winter or a future binge. I closed the door, flipped back the lock, turned, and walked away.

I carry Father's ashes now, potent as peat, sore and rich. I drop a pinch over the red canyon floor. Tiny grey particles sink, sear the earth. A line in the book of ashes.

The western sky promises little that the east hasn't already undergone. My feet curl under, work themselves into the necessary borderlands, nearer the edge. Like Father's paintings, his subjects and stories, his old world maps: Beware! There be lions here! And pirates and magicians and pickpockets; holy fools and angels with missing teeth. Everything has its shadow event, its shifting sands, weightless, going down with the sun.

"Don't do what I did," Father once said. "Go and see the world, goddammit, before the planet forgets who we are."

Now it seems strange, there's a novelty and wisdom within Father's words that are accessible only through my relationship with his remains, his ashes balanced in this leather medicine pouch. Still Life travelling. An emergent property of grief? Or is it joy?

DEATH VALLEY

The mountain bike leans upside down on its seat and handlebars against a rock, spokes ticking, turning on a bright rim of sun. Somewhere in Nevada, on the cusp of Death Valley. A hard, rippling expression of earth and road. Sands going nowhere.

I don't know what to do.

For two days I watch over that bike, as if waiting for its owner, or the repo man. The only other person is the man in the motel/store down the way. He keeps checking me out, standing on his solid porch, shaded, looking out from beneath the brim of his wide blue fedora. I go down there at times, get supplies, a bottle of water, then retreat back to my post, against a rock across from the upside-down bike. Like Jean Valjean pondering a loaf of bread.

"How long do you intend to stay out there like that?" the man in the store asks, flipping back the fedora.

"Don't know," I say.

"Not sure it's legal," he says, "pitching a tent out there. It's not safe either. Spiders, snakes, God knows what else."

"Do you know who owns that bike?"

"Thought you did," the man says, pouring me a glass of juice. "Could be that bike's like manna from the heavens."

"How do you mean?" I ask. I notice the thick, familiar crucifix on the wall, just over the man's shoulder. The San Damiano crucifix, the one that spoke to St. Francis.

"Could be that bike fell off a passing vehicle, one of those RV's," the man says. "Whole lives go missing when a person doesn't use a rear-view mirror."

The desert doesn't laugh. Its humour is bound in a straight face. Sun lines criss-cross the face like exposed riverbeds. Sand blasts dreams.

Each of my steps is placed like a dry shadow turning in the womb of sand. Lovers of fertile grounds come to the desert to witness the void out of which Creation first slipped. Cactus, thick as lungs, bloom at night.

I've heard the eyeball, when removed and suckled, is a good source of protein, or when squeezed can fill a cup with water. I take a pinch of Father's ashes in the palm of my hand. I add a dash of spittle and hold the concoction to the sun, then pour the heated substance over the sand. The ashes blend in, form a surrogate soil.

Father explained to me the power of the Jack pine cone, how it requires fire and wind to help release its seed. How fire bakes the seed until the seed explodes and leaps out into the air. How the wind carries the eager seed toward fresh, charred soils, then lays the seed down. How the seed, like a monk in the desert, digs itself in, penetrates the new life. "The Big Bang articulating itself in a handful of flame and seed," Father said.

It's as if I long for Father's ashes to do the same out here in the desert. As if through Father's ashes a Jack pine will suddenly sprout, weave its trunk and branches, some green shade. The way grief wants things back as they were, that part of grief uncomfortable with itself, so I want to rearrange ecological complexity, ignore planetary becoming, and get my father back.

I've come here for the silence, what the hermit craves. But in this craving there are too many thoughts with fingers fidgeting, pulling furniture across the floor of my mind; tattered laundry on a line, snapping at the earth. Elle spoke of coming to a desert like this, a cleansing. She went north instead, the frozen tundra, winter camped in the Algoma highlands.

"I don't see why I can't come too," I said. My hands were curled around a rubber ball.

"What do you want of me?" she said.

"I just want to be with you," I said. Tighter on the rubber ball.

"What we have needs renewal, solitude," she said.

"Can't we just stay here, in this room?" I said. "Like two pears in a bowl?"

"People go to their chosen mountains and deserts, their caves and wells, just for a taste of something other than themselves," she said. "It's dangerous leaving fruit in a bowl too long."

I tossed the ball against the wall.

Elle took a leave of absence. She had been working for a non-profit organization that advocated and lobbied for more bicycle lanes and protected pathways in the city. An avid cyclist, with the full attire: purple helmet, fingerless leather gloves, a bright yellow wind-resistant Gore-Tex jacket. She joined masses of cyclists and rode in hordes during rush hour, taking up four lanes, pushing traffic back for miles. Critical Mass, they called the protest. With car horns blasting at our backs, drivers yelling, Elle calmed us, insisted we not look back. "Keep riding," she said, "hold your lane and pace. We have every right to be here."

At a red light we were stopped near Queen's Park, about thirty cyclists and other vehicles behind us, impatient engines revving. A woman in her automobile, red-faced, gunned her engine, honked her horn, then suddenly stepped on the gas pedal and ran over the back of Elle's bike. Elle tumbled over, caught between pavement and bike frame, pinned, the car looming over her body. The woman jumped out of her car, screaming at us, hands in the air.

"Look! Look what you've made me do," she yelled.

We converged on her, leaving our lanes. The light turned green, traffic snaked past us as we tended to Elle's fall.

"I'm late for work," the woman insisted, looking down at Elle, noticing the blood on her knee, how it dripped slowly over the pavement, slipped into cracks.

"Well now you're going to be really late," someone said to the woman.

When Elle returned from the northern snows—her retreat, or, as she called it, an advance—the scar on her knee had healed into the shape of a small twig. She believed she had received a deeper call in life.

"The ministry," I said. "Which ministry?"

"The priesthood would be nice," Elle said, grinning. "An overly stacked male clergy could use a good kick in the butt."

"But you know how the Church is," I said, "women in the priesthood and all that."

"That will change," she said, smiling. "Justice grows over time. Five years ago there were no bike lanes in this city, look what's happening now."

She lay back on the floor, staring up at the ceiling.

"The Anglicans will take you," I said. "And the United Church."

"But my roots are in these Catholic soils, for better or worse," she said, slowing her words. "I was standing up there in the north one night, under God knows how many winter stars. I had built a small fire and snowflakes were swirling by and embers and ash were lifting from the firepit and swirling too. It was cold. God, it was cold. And I thought I've stood beneath these stars hundreds of times in my life, but suddenly I felt this pure, naked joy, this stabbing joy of being enfolded by all this free-flowing beauty. And then that line came to me, that line from that book of poetry you gave me by Eckhart. 'If the only prayer you say in your entire life is "thank you," that will be enough.' Yes, I felt that written right into my skin. The lost art of gratitude. As if the Universe is just one, big *Thank You* and everything in life flows from that. Call it a mystical essence, or the communion of saints, the interior sciences, pulling at me. It felt more *real* than real. Just as we dig into the earth for gold and diamonds and oil, there is something of essential worth and shine and energy in this lineage we call Catholic deep within our hearts that must be lifted and lived out in service to the world. Something to ease the suffering. Something of wisdom swimming in the lives of the Francises and the Clares, the Eckharts, the Julian of Norwiches, and now the Mertons and the Keatings, and de Chardin. My goodness, de Chardin. Evolution is not fickle. There is something of illumination here that is necessary for the processes of our being and becoming, our stepping from the known into the unknown, back and forth, again and again, if need be, until we get it! Every moment is pregnant with God."

"So, what are you saying? What do you want to do? Become a nun?"

"No, silly," she said, looking at me. "I just want to serve this realization. I'll start small. Become a psychologist with a mystical bent, and go from there. Maybe I'll write about it if I ever find the words. There are many ways to share in our gifts."

When she returned from her northern desert she was changed, undone by snow and a sense of suffering in the world. I was worried about someone banging at the door, taking her away. Or like St. Peter after the transfiguration, I wanted to keep her all to myself. Build a shelter, stay and pray that the world would change and adapt to us.

But what good is it to pray for the world to change if one is not deep within its restless grasp, its stammering path. Elle said love and prayer had more to do with risk, leaving the heights of revelation and going back into the world. "Put your inner changes into action," she said. "Every generation has to face its suffering anew."

"Remember," she said, sitting up. "We are that unique species that takes care of those who are suffering. We bring flowers to our celebrations, we bring flowers to our birth beds, and we bring flowers to our graves."

What was it? Under a year later we were in the car, driving down the Avenue Road escarpment, a light rain ticking off the windshield. I couldn't feel the temperature dropping, or see the black ice, how it shuddered. Then I noticed Father's hands on her shoulders, handful after handful of scattered street light, ash-grey and diminishing. The spaces between us.

I cannot tell if the lines in the palms of my hands are coming or going. If this road means to flare up or bless.

For too long I've imagined myself a wanderer, member of no gang or belief system, an unmarked animal with eyes and feet fixed on the road. I have been roaming, turning my head away from all I have not wanted to see. So that no one would remember my face. So that wars could come and go, earthquakes, holocausts, famines, the rape of land, man, woman, child, and I'd be nowhere in the midst of the records and documents, photographs and archives. Hidden beneath torsions in the sand. The erosion of time and bone.

How relieved the dead must feel. No longer ashamed of choosing a direction.

I give over my feet to the circular motion of pedalling. Round and round, faster, until the contrasting night shadows of cacti and blowing sands carry me, cut me loose from illusory compulsions. I cannot dream the dead back into being. The night is as black and speckled as a raven's belly.

I leave the mountain bike upside down, on its seat and handlebars, against a rock on the other side of the desert, spokes ticking, turning on a bright rim of sun. Seven a.m.

CITY OF ANGELS

There are those who travel through the desert and over the San Bernardino Mountains and descend into the City of Angels simply to stargaze and look the American Dream in the eye. Others come because the full spectrum of what makes this human journey both tragic and beautiful seems to rise up and greet whatever new light or meaning manages to squeeze through the city's early morning haze. Some arrive at the end of the North American world, their exhaustion seeming most pure.

My feet are moving in other directions, South Central LA, Watts. A reprieve from grief. Baked by the desert, I slide in and take my uneventful place, nothing more to lose. Then a man on his front porch pulls me over for a spot check.

"What you doin'?" he cries.

"Walking, just walking," I say. The first words out of my mouth in weeks.

"Get over here and talk with me, man!"

At times invitations come like the last fruits of a harvest, in odd shapes and sizes, a dusty old apricot. If one walks long enough and far enough, if one's intentions are clear and honest and soaked to the bone in a mossy faith, someone will recognize it. They will get out of their car and cross the highway on foot and leap the fence and go into the orchard and move along the first few rows of trees, and somewhere in the middle of the grove they will find you, ripening there beneath a thick coat of dust. Nothing about you made in China, or south of the border. You're homespun, right off the branch.

"Where you from?" the man asks, coming off his porch, approaching the thick iron fence that surrounds his squat house.

"Toronto," I say.

"Toronto! That's a long walk, man. That's the place where they play baseball in the snow," he says. "I thought maybe you be a cop. You a cop?"

"No, sir."

"You lost?"

"Like I said, I'm just walking. Just looking for the Watts Towers."

"That's back the other way."

"Thanks."

"You on some kind of journey?"

I nod.

"You know where you are?"

"I can smell the ocean, smells like it's thirsty."

"Man, you're a funny one." He laughs and extends his hand over the iron fence, introducing himself as Virgil B.

"Dara," I say.

"Man-o-man." He grins.

We shake hands. He unlocks the iron gate. We sit on his porch, share a beer. We talk about the desert, the heat, the smog. Talk about his time overseas: Nam. Talk about every one of his services as forgotten; not proud for having been in Nam. No one looked him in the eyes for years after he returned. Baby killer, some people called him from the street. That's when he went out into the desert and burned his uniform and buried the ashes in the sand.

"Never felt that kind of pure elation before," Virgil B says. "Never thought I could forgive myself. Never thought God could burst through such a wound."

He leans in.

"Here's the thing," he says. "I went to that war believing I was a good man. Eighteen years old, a young black man and Christian at that. Civil rights just kicking in. All I wanted to do was show that I belonged. So I went. Had to defend our values, our freedoms. And now I'm being trained to kill and I'm loving it, man. I'm loving it. And within weeks I'm in the muck of it, man, I'm watching my buddies get killed and all, and I'm killing too, killing kids my age, older. I'm getting in so close to them, I can see the colour in their eyes, man. And I'm feeling this red-hot passion in me, this thing called rage consuming me, and it's beautiful, not just because of all the death around me, but because I'm doing it, I'm the wild man doing it, and I'm loving it. I'm the bloody Christian wild man doing it . . ."

Virgil B sits back, looking at me.

"So I come back here and suddenly I've got that shock happening, man, that PTSD before they even called it that. I'm back and I'm being called baby killer, and I'm thinking, *Damn right, I'm a baby killer.* I'm a killer through and through, man. That's what I was trained to do. And a Christian killer at that. I kept saying that to myself, kept looking in the mirror and calling myself that, Christian killer, over and over, and that's when I started seeing it, man. I started seeing this crucifix swinging round my neck, and I fell into a kind of spell, a trance. I started seeing that if I was at the actual crucifixion two thousand years ago there'd be a better chance that I'd be the brother hammering the nails into Jesus's feet rather than one of those other brothers and sisters standing by and weeping. And if not that, I'd be handing the damned nails to the brother doing the hammering. Easier to do that than face the truth of my killer soul. It's one thing to wear a shiny crucifix round your neck; it's another thing to know when to pick up your cross and take responsibility for your life. That's the wisdom, man, that's when the truth can set you free. And that's when I went out into the desert and burned my uniform."

Virgil B offers me space in his home. I sleep on a mattress on the floor in a backroom. He gives me a T-shirt and a pair of old jeans. Virgil B works days, two, three jobs. I do the dishes, the laundry, the windows in behind the iron bars which protect Virgil B's home. Virgil B gives me a key to the lock on the iron gate, to the locks on the screen doors, to the locks on the windows, to the locks on the inside door, and to the lock on the barbecue.

"I know," Virgil B says, "it's a lotta locks. Tough 'hood."

Virgil B drives a small yellow-and-purple school bus, drives kids to and from school. In between he takes meals to shut-ins in the neighbourhood, the elderly.

He takes me down to the Mission one day; Virgil B figures about a thousand kids a day trickle over the border into Tinseltown, stars in their eyes, hope in their pockets, but are quickly lost. So the Mission takes them in. "A non-profit, we do what we can," Virgil B says. He greets kids as they come in, gives them bedding, sits with them, and chats away a few hours.

We go down to the county juvenile jail another day. Virgil B knows some of the kids there, neighbourhood kids tripped up and jailed; thieves, dealers, kids of the fist. Virgil B visits the kids weekly, and he brings along a diminutive, sixty-odd-year-old Sister of St. Joseph's, Sister Mary-Margaret. A former native of New York City but for ten years now a full-time resident of the City of Angels. "A change of life," she says, "you just never know what the Lord wants of you." She goes into the jail wearing the full habit, all done up and prehistoric-looking, and she works her gentle spell. The guards lock us up in the room with about twenty hard-core kids all shackled in their orange uniforms, and the sister asks the guards to please unchain the boys. "Could you please unchain the boys today," she says, "just this once?" The guards never comply, they just release a wry, collective grin, then turn away. The sister persists. She speaks with a small, quirky, almost lost voice, the kind of voice one has to look around for, or lean in toward if there's any chance of picking up on its signal. The kind of voice you'd figure the kids would resist or scowl at, make fun of, but the sister prevails, like a cool breeze. "Just watch her," Virgil B whispers to me. And she has the kids' eyes. There's little hunger about the boys when the sister is around, just a sort of indifferent attention, somewhat surprised, as if the black-and-white habit works an opposite effect, doesn't kindle images of an institution all dried and withered but of something almost futuristic, sci-fi, as if perhaps the boys mistake the sister for a Trekkie just beamed in. She tells Gospel stories without the privilege of the pulpit. She weaves words into the modern tongue, places the Prodigal Son and the Good Samaritan on the streets of LA, two jives guys she calls them, out and about, swaggering, gettin' high, sleeping in parks, shooting hoops, and eventually gettin' rolled and losing everything to the Insatiable Pigs. There is a sense the sister means the police when she says pigs; she kind of leaves the word *pigs* dangling and open to interpretation, in the way Jesus left his words dangling and open; so many meanings available, one could be arrested and crucified for just about anything. The boys seem to recognize a little of themselves in the words, lifting their eyes at the sound of *pigs*, rattling their chains. There were no dramatic St. Paul conversions there, not one of the boys ever breaks out into the sweat of repentance; that isn't the sister's intention. Her idea is to tell the stories, over and over again if need be. "Just sowing seed," she says.

Sunset Boulevard. We're witness to the glittering aftermath of a three-car pileup. Two Mercedes and a pickup truck full of fruits and vegetables have collided, metals and fruits scattering across the road. No one is hurt. Drivers and passengers await the police, swap phone numbers, insurance companies, speak of whose fault lies where.

Chaos theorists suggest that the flutter of a butterfly wing in China could set off a chain of atomic events which could eventually lead to a storm brewing in the Black Forests of Germany or a collision all the way around the globe in California. If I wail in a red canyon or across the streets of a downtown core, does it ripple outward to become a snowfall in the north or a prairie drought? If a lover turns with a weapon on a beloved, can the lover blame their actions on the ripple effect of a butterfly wing in China?

Was I ever in control of that car, the steering wheel in my hands? The crack of a collision without conscience, mouths drying up. When once beneath the ripple of her hair I lay like a wing.

Simon Rodia spent over thirty years plying his craft and sweat to the Watts Towers, Michelangelo in his blood. His muscles taut and crackling, a speechless music to his hands. Like strange, hollowed cathedrals, the eight slightly bent towers jut out of the neighbourhood, rise like a testament of the heart, a maddening rhythm of tile and glass. It's the lull and hum inside meditation I feel here. Mortar and cement, broken seashells, laid out like a permanent offering. My mind pauses, a fork in the road. At the end of the known world, at the end of a continental drift. The energy inside these tongue-like structures bursts out, leaps conventions, all naked and gleaming. Something in my own body is preparing to leap from the world of convention too.

Virgil B and I get down on our knees on the pavement before the Watts Towers, our intention without distraction.

We talk about our fathers, their hands, the things they made. The things they left unsaid. I take a small pinch of Father's ashes and give a gentle portion to Virgil B, palms upturned and shining with ash.

"My father was afraid of fire," Virgil B says. "He was never the same after Hitler's war. It left him tongue-tied, man. All he could do was hammer and build, hammer and build half the homes round here. When his hands swelled with arthritis, when just a subtle vibration set off the pain, he didn't know what to do, how to adjust to being still. When I found him in the kitchen a few years ago, lying on the floor, I knew he was dead right away. I'd seen enough dead bodies to know. But he looked at peace, for the first time in years. I don't know how he did it, but he did. Like he was in that deep peace of sleep, man. You know the one, where there's nothing to identify with, all pain gone. Maybe that's all heaven is, man, that deep peace of sleep. Maybe it's closer to us than we allow ourselves to know. Maybe."

"My father dreamed in fire," I say. "He and my mother made a pact, thinking they'd die together, like true lovers, I guess. They didn't plan on the cancer getting her first."

"Her remains?"

"Ashes too. But buried in her parents' plot," I say. "I swear, when her ashes touched down, I felt something in my chest fading out and flaring at the same time."

We turn our palms over, watch Father's ashes drift and settle beneath the Towers. White ash on black earth. Indelible as moss; carbon-rich.

I look out over the Pacific. Waves press into the shoreline, salt my bare feet. Dark seafoam stops just short of my knees. A piece of driftwood slips up the beach. Mussels flicker over jagged rock, halo-like; big sun going down. I lift my water-logged legs. Sometimes it's the direction that chooses you, waves lead back out, pulling at your shirt sleeve like a tour guide: this way please.

Virgil B gives me a straw hat and a pair of sandals, shaded blue like dusk over the ocean.

"I have a feelin' it's hot where you're headed."

Our embrace seems weightless. A still spot.

"Thanks . . . *gracias* . . . *merci* . . . what more can I say?"

Flying thousands of feet above the turning planet, the North American continent recedes from view. All its traffic and snares and dietary plans for survival: gone.

It's difficult to reconcile sleep and dreams. Night waters waver below, reach and loom. The pull of another wave. So much space, such uncertainty. All the words, the studies in religion and art, a career in education, the simplicity of Elle's touch and love; what seemed most precious to me is no longer a viable means of expression. I am mute before the Maker. There is no vow worth heeding.

I'm aware there's another body of water within me, larger than the ocean waters, looming, and terrifying too. I'm moving into a world not mine, what the mystics might call *taking leave of God.*

VITI LEVU

Fiji. The island of Viti Levu. It opens to me like a wing, like a lover undressing from the eyes down. Its shorelines and hillsides and undisguised leaves give me suckle. Its fields provide space for all that is dormant and fallow and unknown. It welcomes the stranger, sits him in its circle, pours its great root-drink into a dark, wooden bowl, takes up its cup and presents it to its guest, clapping the deep-tongued clap of its hands as the guest drinks of its gracious source.

With each clap the metaphysical world opens out; with each sip of kava I sink into a place of original being.

Deep in Fiji's drink a polished grace prevails, an underground poetry. I don't know if that is its intention, but as I reflect upon its soils and wells, its kava and fish, its ankle bracelets and trysts, I see this dying-to-be-born-again is no longer a diminishment but a deepening, a movement into blue-in-green.

Nadi. I walk the dust roads of this primal town. I follow the mysterious odours, the diesel, the sugar cane, pressed silk fabrics, garlic, the curried fish, meats and vegetables, and rare spices. I pass through the outdoor market, the centre of exchange. Withered fruit peelings strewn on the damp ground. I see the Fijian women with the large bellies and the dark dimpled smiles, a telling glance. I hear the stories of their children lost to the dengue fever and the bite of the mosquito which has been ravaging the island for over a year. The women are seated at tabletops decorated with trinkets and cassava and fruit descended from the moon. Surviving children sit on the ground behind their mothers, roll bruised dice and play with rusted jacks. I turn to the men with the canes and bent legs, the gnashes in their cheeks, their bodies spun in tides and fields. The men are sitting in the shade, under the only tree in a vacant lot. I step up, the alien kid flown in. I laugh at the thought of a plane and time and space, things flying and landing, cutting through the heavens. I ask about work, a place to apply my hands. The men smile and bang their canes, raise half arms. The time for sugar cane is months away, they say, the Brits would never harvest the stuff for themselves, had to bring over our Indian brothers and sisters at the turn of the century and rearrange our lives and local economies, but you're welcome, son, to lend a hand out there in the fields. The pay is crap but you'll be fed a bowl of rice and the spicy stuff, three times a day, and you'll have a hut to sleep in, a place to lay your head. You'll have to eat with your hands and shit in a hole, there's no toilets out there in the fields, and nothing to wipe your ass with either, so you'll have to use a splash of water and your fingers. You'll learn about your life, kid. God is in the mess.

I take the windowless bus up the coast to the north of the island, through Lautoka, the ocean riding the rim out of the corner of my eye. Village after village, I'm part of the human cargo. My breath has equal weight with the dust in the air.

In Ba I'm met by a young man, the son of the farmer I'm to work for. The son greets me, takes my packsack, shoulders it, and leaves me with the impression that he'd sell all its contents if it meant he could get ahead. But we walk on; we've got two hours of road ahead, so best get on with it, pay attention to the step, and cover my head from the sun. As we walk the young man tells me he dreams of North America, its wealth and TV. He's animated, excited, walking backwards, facing me as we walk. Is it true? he persists. Are you rich? I smile, feeling the old life at my back, all I've left. The young man turns toward the road. He looks at the ocean as if at a finger shaking in his face.

The working farm is in the hills, encircled by twists of mangrove trees. The homestead is made up of four or five tin huts, a grass hut, a chicken coop, a fenced-in area for two oxen, and a small closed-in area to shit. I'm to sleep in a tin hut with the young man and his two brothers, on a straw bed with a mosquito net hanging over my head. I'm told many people have died over the year from the bite of the mosquito, a rare disease which is transmitted, so best get wrapped in that net. It's the bite in the night that might get me and I wouldn't even know it. I'd wake with a fever and after that everything would be a blur.

Upon arrival we're greeted by the young man's sisters. They meet us as we come over the hillside and escort us to the homestead where they serve us tea laced with sugar. I'm invited to sit with the whole family in a circle on a straw mat; the father, the mother, the three sons, and two daughters. They want to know of my travels, eyes keen. I tell them about the soils and streets of an old life, of Great Lakes, of a lover whose death pulls my heart, of Father's ashes, how I carry him and mean to give him to the world; how for years I've been walking without lifting an eye and only now am I learning to step with my vision linked with the horizon's curve.

The family claps their hands, they nod, sit back, and drink of their tea and fresh kava. They slip through tens of thousands of years to tell me of their gods and goddesses, Shiva and Vishnu and Brahma. They speak of forest temples where rivers guide their myths over stone and shale, the currents of their faith. As dusk approaches and the volcanic soils begin to settle, the young men take me by the arm and lead me down the hill into the sugar cane fields. We find a well, we strip down, the young men call me brother and laugh out loud at my body, white as the moon. We bathe together, pour water over one another, lather ourselves up and wash ourselves down. The water is day warm. I can hear a rippling motion inside the well, so many underground currents, looming within.

I'm here to work but I'm a guest as well. Apart from tending the sugar cane fields, bending close to their sweet roots, I'm not to lift a hand around the homestead. I'm escorted and accompanied most everywhere I go, treated as if I'm something rare. At night I sit on the straw mat near the huts, playing cards, drinking the root drink, relaxing, thoughts supple as fruit on a bough. And I think back upon that first night and the ritual of every day and night since, the rising at six, the cold waters over my face and through my hair, the hot hours of sun, my hands in the fields, of work and the magnetic pull of life down under the equator, how water curls clockwise round my belly and eyes. That first night, as on all nights, I take my lantern and follow the young men to our hut, for a brief moment covering the lantern with my hand and looking deep into the night skies. I soak in the constellations, the shadows between stars, the fearless strains of dark matter. I sense that half of my being and blood not yet uncovered or conceived or blessed. The Southern Cross whispers like blinking coals beneath the last of the night's flame. Beneath the mosquito net, after the young men have said "goodnight, brother," and blown out their lanterns, I can hear the pull of their breaths and the fumbling with their bodies as they play with themselves in the dark. I touch my lips, murmuring an old prayer which has emerged after years fallow within my body, the prayer Mother whispered in those rare days of her faith. She prayed as if from a previous life, a cloistered cell, "Lord Jesus Christ, have mercy on me." She repeated it over and over again until it seemed she was drunk on the prayer. I sense the ancient roads the prayer has taken to reach my lips, layers of soils fortifying each word.

The road will take you on your own. That is essential. It is essential in a civilization bent on crowding you out. To find that travelling solitude in which your body rings like grasses, brilliant with dew.

The young man with the North American dream notices something in me and gives me a polished gem to carry with me on my way. The gem is wrapped in blue tissue paper. He gives me the gift on the day I find him in our hut, rummaging through my things. He is wearing my T-shirt and blue jeans, standing before the mirror in the manner of an undersized John Wayne, half surprised and half shocked at himself. I sit with him and watch as he sifts through poses, running the full gamut from Chuck Heston to Woody Allen. "Nothing fits," he says, the clothes falling from his body like rain. He gives me the gem because he wants an aspect of himself to accompany me on the way. As a final gesture I stand with the family in a circle near the chicken coop and sprinkle a pinch of Father's ashes over the beautiful black earth there, bestowing the elegant mark of a life no longer borrowed or abandoned.

I walk. Four days I've been on the road, further into the north of Viti Levu. I find a place of refuge under the trees, on the rim of the ocean. It's nowhere and it's everywhere and gradually I'm aware that I'm here to weather the blue, the storm inside. I've got rice, vegetables, and the spicy stuff. I've got a hut, a well with fresh water, an ocean with plenty of fish. My body has become a tuning fork. My sleep is deep, undisturbed. The days widen. I wake at six, stretch my limbs, the thin ropes of my arms. I draw a circle in the sand near the pull of tides. I sit in the circle for hours on end, light tracing my chest, my sleeping heart. All I had deferred arises with the sun's arc.

For three days and nights I sit in the ritual circle, eyes closed, breathing. I know the sun is near, burning white. I sense the power of each night, an incarnate darkness. It's been days since I've had anything to eat. The tides approach and brush my feet, run up my legs. I sink back into the belly of the wet sand, engulfed by the tide's rush. I open my eyes and the storm within breaks through, shudders and pours forth; the old life I failed. All I must shed. All the sin and shit and snow, the weathers I've used to close the heart. All the automobiles and roads, the black ice, the elements, oncoming trucks skidding, sliding, their brakes locking. Elle and Father, gone. Mother too. Shame lodged in my right foot. Anger like a drug taking me down. When everyone who has ever mattered to me has slipped from the world, where is forgiveness? My right foot suffered the disconnection, and no amount of strength or prayer or faith could move the car into safety, out of the dip, the ice, to the side of the road. How my body survived, I don't know. I remember Elle, the car so still, the weather a weapon. I'm pulled back by loss. The gravity of a lover, a father, a mother; the self.

How can I recoil when every one of my tears is working through the seams with their own peculiar passion, loneliness and mortification, the art and science of certain emotions? Who is this self that suffers and weeps?

Moonlight laps in my hands.

PILGRIM

I head south to the capital, Suva. My senses disrobe. I hear the bartering of voices, live animals, the tilt of market scales. The jingle of four ankle bracelets across the road and the coo of a babe in a woman's arms. I follow my grief for a sound.

I take a room in the hotel where the woman works. There are three sagging beds, a wash basin, a frayed towel, and a window with a long view of the harbour. Ships are anchored against the bulging tides.

I sit quietly on a chair by the open window.

I hear clients in their chosen rooms where the curtains have faded into orange and the light bulbs have been dimmed. Looking over the harbour, the streets are as fluid as the ocean. I watch as a procession of men arrive by night, hats slanted, hands concealed, toothpicks extended from mouths. Into the early morning I listen to their cheap proposals, their premature ejaculations. The demand for more, and less.

The lost sleep of 3 a.m. I've smuggled my own bent body here, like the ancients who carried relic bones of the saints beneath thick black cloaks, town to town, to prove belief. Faith without flesh.

Four nights into sitting still. The woman rolls an orange along the hallway floor, slides sweating peels under my door. I've come here because of an ache buried deep in my thoughts. Because of the counter-revolution of a root working through a grave.

So, during the night I cross the boundary line of my breath and step into her life. My bare feet lift through orange peels to a room where the mirrors on the walls have been removed. Her four ankle bracelets rub against the sheets. Her welcome on my arm is like a torch.

The bed is a landscape where violence does not reign. She offers me the kava, then the wine. She asks me to hold her child close to my chest. She knows what the sound of a heartbeat can do for a little one's sense of belonging. I lie with her at my side and the child asleep on the pillow. I sink into the finger hole of candlelight between the dark curve of her hip against my thigh.

Once my body knew the pulse of another's dream and sex, Elle's sacred sweat. Now here, in the hum of another world, another pulse, there is the unexpected scent of another woman's hair. Pine tar and aloe. I savour the myth of her flesh, the scarred breast, the four folds of her belly. I laugh at the manner in which I can't make love, the wisdom of my impotence. All along I've mistaken life for what rises, a wing and some waves, and now there's nothing more to raise within myself. The great religions of the world struggle in their bell towers, ignoring words like soul, rivulet, autumn, bracelet.

The grace of her breath and the tension of my many unresolved desires. To mourn, like a literature carved into stone, is an elegant work of time.

I offer her a pinch of Father's ashes. She wets her index finger, dips it in the ash, and traces it upon the scar which is her lost breast. Later she rubs wet ash along the twist and ache of my right foot, where the stubborn pulse of an old collision still stirs.

When I wake at eight, she and the child are gone. The room is gleaming. My head is thick with the effects of kava and bad wine. She has cleaned my wallet and my pockets of all cash and privilege.

I give up my demand on the future. I do not pretend to know where it is I'm headed, why or to what end.

SOUTHERN STAR

The South Pacific circles, goes under, then unfolds again from the inside out. A repeating gesture, unashamed and without worry.

In the thickening blue-green waters, in the glancing scent of salt, my body's ignorant half descends, prepares its strange uninitiated limbs, its hidden language, blind like music. There are no mountains here, no wild heights, yet I feel the clutch of vertigo.

These haunting, beautiful waters.

I find work on a small cargo ship that hauls material goods from island-nation to island-nation; Western Samoa, Tonga, New Caledonia. I go days without showering, endure night sweats and dreams distinguished by their absence of fresh water and roads.

All us working men, sleeping in cabins without portholes, our defiant lives. Or leaning in steel corners, two or three bodies greased and lonely, moving to the grind of the engines below. A bucking, seething love. All of us, an unmarked cargo rocking toward a holy star.

"You don't say much," one of the ship's hands says to me, eyes gritty and direct, his hands blackened by grease.

We stand under the midday sun, bodies rock-hard from all manner of manual labour. The ship sways, pushing us up against each other. My companion moves back against the railing, wipes his brow, loosens the top button of his shirt. A small silver crucifix swings out, shiny and moist with clinging sweat.

"There's that bit in the Bible," my companion says. "The one about how from the fullness of the heart the mouth speaks."

I nod.

Then it happens.

Out of the corner of my eye I catch sight of a humpback whale, smooth and shining, immense. And then not one, but two, and three, and four other whales spouting water, sharp, almost fierce, hot-blooded, massive bodies pulling the ocean through their quickened flesh.

It is a shock to my system, the whole of the civilized world falls apart. For weeks I become silent. In the face of such a vision, such grandeur, what I know or what I thought to be the wisdom of my age, means nothing, has come to nothing. I am back to ground zero, square one. The first breath.

I wash up on the crooked shores of New Zealand, like a great chunk of driftwood soaked to the core; its bark stripped, its trunk fire-gouged, charred, and hollowed out. It's springtime in the northern hemisphere but it's kicking up autumn down here, reds and yellows descending.

Give it all up, I think. Everything. Everything that does not hold to truth. Everything I've identified with: a son, a lover, a teacher, my race, my colour, my sex. All these wild experiments and specimens, all that I've used to mix and match to make a Man; pour it all into the bitter compost. Archaic Man, Medieval Man, Renaissance Man, Modern Man, Postmodern Man, stir it all up, and see what emerges. It isn't the cold waters that grip, nor the thrill of a night sky full of underworld stars, nor a New Zealand dawn which strikes like an arrow and causes a shudder. No. It's not the kiss of a woman which stirs me but the dream of a snake, something ancient and coiled at the base of my spine which suddenly bites my ass and draws black blood. I sit up in the waves and look at my driftwood body as with a broken lover's gaze. Even this has to go. All is in ashes. Even my name.

So I rise to my feet and walk the north island, I leave Auckland and head south. My body is a sieve, I'm shaking and shaking. I'm going down through the years and layers and weeds and roots. My navel is screaming. Brain cells quiver. Deep in my skin, deeper in my blood. Truth is painful. If I don't travel yet deeper, flesh is just flesh, and the stars would have no business sinking roots in our navels.

I stand before the small arch of the Southern Star Abbey, face to face with the silence. Hardly able to speak of my needs, or bring my thoughts together into a coherent whole, I manage to ask for time and space in a small cell, plug myself into a hole in the world and contemplate all the things I am not. Father Daniel recognizes what I cannot see: the climate of my mind, and the unpolished shine behind my eyes.

I ask about meditation. How to do it? What's the trick?

"Tricks, there are no tricks," Father Daniel says, looking me in the eyes. "But, please, tell me about your practice?"

"I don't have one."

"I see," Father Daniel says. "Come with me then. We'll have a cup of tea, we'll sit on the porch, and watch the clouds come and go."

Weeks, months, glimmer.

Father Daniel has me step into the simplicity of each day. I work the fields, I tend the cattle, I fix broken fences, I take rusted nails out of old boards and emotions, I prune the evergreen hedges; I learn to step delicately over the down-under autumn furrows.

Each afternoon I'm encouraged to take a walk into the backwoods. I follow the long shadows of cloud cover and the pull of a distant mountain peak in the west. Each day I walk alongside a stream that meanders through the woods and narrows into a bracken pond. Its waters are still and black and unreflecting. I sit on a rock, looking and listening. I don't know how long I sit there by the pond, each afternoon, eyes silent and listening, but there's something in the stillness, a lucidity that goes to the guts of my soul, that if I were in a canoe and were to dip my paddle, I'd be breaking an ancient vow.

After weeks of working and walking and sitting with morning brew and watching the clouds come and go, I'm invited to spend time and space with Father Daniel, cultivating methods of prayer and meditation. Or as he says, learning to resonate with the Presence of God. A stout, gentle man, eyes so clear, I find myself questioning everything untapped within myself. Like any novice, I insist I want to pray and meditate like him, to open the heart like him, to love as he seems to love. And like any good teacher he tells me in his own quiet way *to shut up*.

"You want to be like me without having to be yourself," he says. "Your true, unique, and shining self."

We sit quietly each morning for an hour. He has me rock my upper body side to side, like a metronome, then back to front, as I slowly align my posture and come to a gentle and centred stop. Neck straight, mouth slightly open, hands in lap, palms facing upwards. He encourages me to take up a mantra. Maranatha. To place it upon my tongue, to breathe in and through each syllable, in and out, in and out, for forty breaths. Ma-Ra-Na-Tha. The sweet Aramaic tongue of Jesus. So this we do, together, in the power and ease of our shared being, sharing this mantra. Starting aloud, then sinking into the quiet of our breathing. If a thought or an itch arises, I'm instructed to quietly tune back into the mantra and my breath. I find myself lifting and sinking at the same time, bathed in an unnameable silence.

"Ma-Ra-Na-Tha . . ." Come, Lord . . .

Then one morning Father Daniel says, "Drop the mantra."

I fall silent, stumble over the prayer's intent. So accustomed to the rhythm and breath and elegance of the mantra I've become.

Father Daniel speaks softly, planting his contemplative seeds.

"From time to time it is necessary to put the mantra down and anchor yourself in the gift of your awareness. Even the mantra is an object to which we can attach ourselves and become dependent. Notice how the mantra, like a word or a thought, a concept or a belief, or just the view outside this window, simply arises in your awareness, as easy as clouds passing over blue sky. Become less preoccupied then with the objects of experience and more interested in that which is aware of experience. The Seer, and not the seen."

I continue to sit quietly, sinking back, listening.

Morning after morning.

"In the grief there is silence, yes. Strangely, when we fall in love we are speechless. A similar felt silence. Savour this. Be gentle with grief. Think of it as a stringed instrument that requires fine tuning. Not too tight, nor too loose.

"It is written we are made in the image and likeness of God. What if we actually lived like this? What would it mean to live as the tender and unique and divine masterpiece you are? What would you be willing to risk of yourself? What truth? Jesus was killed for risking to live his life as a child of God. It was called blasphemy to do so. What if the true blasphemy of the heart is *not* to live as a child of God?

"I give you these gifts to help you in your navigation of grief's terrain, the mountains and valleys of this sacred encounter. Grief left unattended can make one reckless. Mountain work is good and hard and necessary. It is also essential to return to the valley and do the good and hard work of love and healing. Because the world is in pain and needs you. For now, if sitting quietly and focusing on your breath and the mantra is the call, then do so. Make that disciplined practice. If sitting quietly and soaking in the inexhaustible beauty of life just as *it is* is the moment's call, then do so. Sitting or walking, baking bread or building a house; eyes closed or wide open, whether in solitude or serving the lives of others, live your life as a prayer. If God is singing a song of creation and you in your intrinsic giftedness are one word in that Divine chorus, each of us responsible for lifting our one, unique word, such that if one of us is missing, God's song would be incomplete, what word would you be?"

Silence.

I begin to weep, daily, back in my room after our morning sit.

Three a.m. Night winds gather towards a new moon. Starlight angles across bare branches, bark white, purpling against the cool night sky. Sloping trunks gleam, shades of the prehistoric. The unnamed. Thickened leaves over the forest floor support the world above.

Life down under the equator is a story being told in reverse. Last lines are first lines, the seasons flowing back through themselves. I am strengthened by loss. Graves are delivery rooms, passageways, wombs where stone is rubbed against stone, sending up sparks which the stars above look down upon. They chart the way.

How many thoughts like clouds have come and gone in my lifetime? How many sensations? How many beliefs? How often have I clung to a *belief* like a life raft, afraid that if I drifted beyond the horizon line of my certainty I'd disappear into a world of waves? And how often have the foundations of my beliefs eroded or burnt away regardless of whether I have crossed the horizon line or not? That I'd be with Elle forever; that I'd walk Father through to old age and bury him with Mother. That I'd happily teach English or history, the arts and humanities, until the tender age of fifty-five. That I'd retire and Elle and I would travel. That we'd purchase an insurance policy that would guarantee that freedom and promise. That we'd pass that policy onto our children. That we'd welcome their children into our beautiful life. So much has come and gone; the magic spark of childhood, the cool fury of adolescence. All this dying. How can I be certain of what I believe now when each wave is a hole of loss as vast as an ocean and my craft is so small and fragile? There's a lodestar amongst the constellations, yes, but what's this in my hand: A rudder or an oar?

The days and nights here are punctuated by the Liturgy of the Hours. Lauds, vespers, early morning vigils. We sing Psalms; the Universe knows we mean no harm. Father Joseph, eighty-two years young, a suitor of light and bells that sound off in the mind, takes me aside one night after prayer and asks of my intentions. Will I stay and become a monk, a priest, a brother of the vine? Standing under the stars, I cannot answer. But my feet twitch at the thought, and Father Joseph says he understands.

For this I no longer worry about my unresolved path.

Is it history that chooses its moment of catharsis, or the mind that clings to the hard work of time, shattered glass, the eternal wrestling match?

When word reaches us that the Berlin Wall is coming down, Father Daniel retrieves an old black-and-white television set from the storage room and sets it up in the common room. Father Joseph prepares a pound cake and tea, and all the monks and guests sit still and poised on old couches and chairs, backs straight, anticipating one of those rare and edifying moments for which they had been praying. Brother Barnabas, of Irish-German descent, sits, hands folded in his lap, and suggests that, as a Cistercian community, we honour silence and watch the televised moment with the sound turned down. The others agree. So we sit, down under the known world, where history is less concerned with its own image, and watch as thousands of small, restless bodies hammer away at fortified walls, tearing bricks and barbwire from their foundations, rubbing the ink and paint of graffiti from their fingertips, until everything that once seemed impenetrable and etched in the psyche, comes crashing down.

An unbound quiet fills the room. Mid-spring here, kicking in autumn north of the equator. I smudge the television screen with a dampened fingertip of Father's ashes. Even the ashes come crashing down.

Standing beneath the arch of the abbey, Father Daniel and I give our goodbyes, bowing to one another, then embracing.

Thank you. *Gracias. Merci.*

There's so much more I could say. I just don't have the words.

CAPTAIN BILL'S

Sydney.

The night flight was smooth and clear. There was little turbulence. My body didn't resist sleep. When we landed I placed my hand upon the warm tarmac and bowed my head.

It is a hot December day. Green leaves hold themselves against a blue, blue morning sky. Ocean waters lift and move about freely in the hydrosphere. Antarctic winds, interior desert winds, winds like drumming dreams, travel about. The sun getting in under my scalp, burning clean.

Father. Elle. It's been a year.

I kiss the ground. Give thanks. God is in the tears.

Father Daniel has given me the address of an ex-monk, now a restaurateur. Once known as Brother Nathan, now known as Bill, or Captain Bill as he likes to call himself. He's a big, round man with red cheeks, deep blue eyes, and greying blond hair pulled back into a pirate's ponytail. He takes my hand and presses into it, pulling me closer. He gets a whiff of my body's odour, my hair, sea salt, the imprints of where I've been. The ocean behind my eyes.

"In the end I didn't really trust the monastic life," he says, his voice quick and certain. "But then I wasn't a very good monk. A chaser of clouds, I think that's what your friend Father Dan would say of me."

He winks and pats his belly, letting go of my hand.

"So, you need work, is that it?"

"If there's something available, yes."

"In this business," he says, "there's always something available."

I take up the quiet life: work in the restaurant, cooking, waiting tables, washing dishes. I sleep in a small room in the basement and stay with the discipline of sitting quietly each morning and afternoon, sourcing the silence. There is a vibrancy within the grief now as if I am sitting on the verge of a new language. At times it requires me to kneel.

Captain Bill's. An upgraded, fancy hamburger joint. Real red meat. Twelve ounces of the stuff cooked over an open grill. Seating capacity, thirty-six persons. Black tabletops, chrome legs, squeaky wooden chairs angled over a hardwood floor. Jazz on the stereo; Miles Davis, Ellington, Chet Baker. "I love things American," the captain says, "though I've never been." The imported dream.

Everyone takes their hamburgers seriously, religiously. One customer always takes my hand when he orders and tells me how he likes his burger:

"Very, very burnt," he says. "Black to the core, not the slightest hint of juice. And I'd like my relish heated, very, very hot."

He pats the back of my hand and sends me off, me and the silence.

Most customers want their burgers medium-rare, nothing too fancy, and a salad instead of French fries, a diet cola instead of the real thing. Everyone watching their waistlines. Captain Bill assures those most concerned about their waistlines that his meat is lean, very lean; no weight gained, nothing lost. He runs a tight, balanced ship.

Until the captain begins missing the daily grind. He shows up at the end of the night to see how much money is in the till. He pays his respects to certain quasi-influential customers, makes the rounds, pats his working crew on the back, then raids the cash register, and gives his farewells like a sailor of the high seas pulling away from shore. And off he sails into a late night on a binge of booze, young men and women, and Chinese food. This he relates to me, over the weeks, as if I have become his Father Confessor. Eventually he becomes a no-show when we really need him; as in, there's no gas for the stove, or a food supplier shows up with a bill two months overdue and we have no money in the till, and I have to stall, make up excuses, say the boss man will most definitely be in tomorrow, tomorrow, tomorrow . . . At best the captain runs the ship via the phone, from the comfort of his bed. From there he fills me in on the details of his late-night adventures, his sexual trysts, ignoring my plea for cash to pay the bills. "Don't worry," he sings, "be happy." Humming through the phone receiver. Bobby McFerrin himself.

Slowly other workers begin disappearing as well, or not showing up for their shifts. Pay-cheques bounce, the captain is indisposed, a gradual diminishment of place. There are days and nights when I'm on my own, taking orders, cooking meals, serving, cleaning up, and cashing out. Somehow, through the silence, through will and sweat, I survive the rushes, relying on a deeper rhythm of the heart.

One night things come to a head. I cannot keep up with the rush, the stream of customers coming through the doors. Like a conductor without his music sheets and a band gone wild. So I close up shop early, sun on an incline, holding its gaze. After cleaning up, I take a dozen green garbage bags full of trash out to the curbside for the nightly pickup. But this trash adds up to nothing but unconsumed foods, chunks of French fries, lettuce leaves, gutted tomatoes, half-chewed buns, meat bits, bones; unfinished desserts, pies, cakes; empty cartons of milk, creamers, ice cream; crumpled paper napkins, coffee grinds and filters, wet herbal tea bags, pop bottles, crushed cans; everything clinging and clang-ing, a busted-up Santa sack. I stand there, looking up and down the block, eyeing these green garbage bags stuffed full and sitting on the curbside. About twenty-five restaurants in the area, clear up the block, and all our trash out in front, waiting. The glory and shame of waste. I suddenly imagine my children's and their children's world, covered, steeped in heaps of ghostly green garbage bags, like body bags, like bags full of withering autumn leaves.

The following night I can hardly get my body to function at work. For every dish prepared and served, at least half of the meal is left on the plate, untouched. The hamburgers are huge, with names like Manhattan or Vegas, smothered in rich cheeses and spears of broccoli and layers of hand-cut mushrooms. The French fries are as big as four-wheel drives, hand-cut too. I watch people eat, form mouths around twelve ounces of oozing meat, an awkward wrestling match between insatiable opponents, between bellies and burgers and eyes hooked on an economic boom time. I wonder, where does it all go? Where is it going? *Where is it all going?*

A week later there are just two of us working the burger ship. Ana, a runaway from Mother Russia, trying, as she says, to get as far away as possible from totalitarian politics, waits tables while I cook and clean up. Ana, always with a smile, a soft gait as she walks, hair dark and luxurious, clearing my mind. A space on a windowsill.

The waste slowly builds up, compiling itself at my back, even though I have been quietly cutting back on portions. Feeling frustrated again, eyeing the mound of waste and imagining my kid's voice coming from somewhere inside the mess until I can't recognize the voice anymore, I think of chucking the job, the work, the faint prayer inside, when there is a knock on the emergency exit door next to the open grill. I open the door and there, standing, is a short, solid, heavy-bearded man, planted like rhubarb. At first I think he is mistaken, but he immediately asks if I have any spare food. He'll gladly take the scraps. Ana is standing beside me.

"It's only one man," she says into my ear. "And not a lineup like the ones I've known back in the Old World."

I ask the man to wait a minute and Ana and I gather a few scraps, a fresh salad, bread, and give them to the man, his eyes an unattainable horizon. He says a kind thank you, a God bless, and bows away.

The next night he's there again, knock knocking, with a friend in tow.

"Any scraps?" he asks.

This goes on for a week or so. It becomes common for some of the people in the street to knock on the emergency exit door three times when I am working the grill. Knock three times, wait, and knock again.

One night Captain Bill shows up, takes me aside, pulling in Ana as well.

"What's going on here?"

He's heard rumours, he's seen people in the streets eating half-heated burgers and mangled French fries that look vaguely familiar to him. His meat.

"Scraps," I say.

"It's got to stop," he says, an eyebrow raised.

"But it's taking care of the waste," Ana says. "We're not really losing anything."

"It's the cost factor," the captain says. "And for insurance reasons. Some guy out there chokes on my food and they trace it back here and I get sued and lose my business . . . I'll be sunk."

That night the captain comes into the restaurant and spends the whole evening in the prep area making pies, hovering like a hawk. When the knock knocking comes like a sound out of heaven, the captain is the first to the emergency exit door. He springs it open, quickly, and announces to the five men gathered there, "That's it! No more handouts!" This happens three more times that night, the knock knocking, the captain answering the door, the blunt rejection, and the surprised, hungered look on the face of a stranger.

The next night is the same situation, the captain hovering, watching, making sure I don't waver. There are a few knocks on the emergency exit door, but this time the captain doesn't respond. He leaves the door bolted, barricaded with boxes of lettuce and large bags of French fries.

People pass the front of the restaurant, glancing in, sometimes waving, or seeking out their own reflection in the large picture windows, adjusting their image and moving on. But on this night, eight or nine of the ex-back-door patrons stand there, facing the large windows, looking in at me behind the open grill, their shoulders squared, hands in pockets. The captain begins a curious sweat at the forehead.

One of the men makes a move, a quiet, harmless move. Unlocking his shoulders, removing hands from his old overcoat pockets, he approaches the entrance to the restaurant, steps in through the door, and stands there as if nothing in the world could defeat him, would defeat him on this night. Not the heat, not the hunger, not the day-in day-out sweat of life in the streets. Customers are catching on to the scene at the window and to the man standing in their midst, his body swaying now, searching for the strength to carry on, as if he had grown used to a hard wind holding him up all his years and now here, protected by three walls and a fourth full of windows, there is no wind to lean on. His eyes become quietly direct. He returns the same stare with which he knows he is being stared at.

The ole captain stands back on his heels, looking at me, looking to Ana, looking to the man in the doorway, looking to the faces of his favoured customers, awaiting the verdict. The lone man stands, his clothing loose, weather-worn, shaped by the elements. His companions at the window loosen up, send a silent, psychic message to their comrade. A pause. Captain Bill seizes the pause, steps forward, and signals for me. He holds me at the upper arm, squeezes, and whispers into my ear, "This is your mess."

Now the man stands like a small child, a pup, eyes moist. My heart pounds, my body aware of a deeper call. I can sense the captain at my back, his penetrating glare, hard, cold pins. And the customers, waiting on me, their meals going cold. Do something, will you? The lone man and me, now eye to eye, our breaths circling close.

Ana approaches. She asks the man, "Do you need any help?"

"Why don't you answer the door anymore?" he asks.

"I'm sorry," I say. "It's not our restaurant . . . our food . . ."

"Just a bite," he says, "that's all we're asking for."

Ana looks at me, then back to Captain Bill, the customers, the open grill, the smell of fresh-cooked burgers. She turns back to the man, puts her small hand on his shoulder, and guides him to the first empty chair. If he wants a bite, he'll get a bite. And the others at the window? Come on in, Ana and I wave. And in they come, one by one, and we seat them, pulling together tables enough to seat them as one company, seven in all.

The captain steps back, turning peach yellow and red, sweating.

"Who the hell is going to pay for this?"

"Don't worry," Ana says, looking at me. "We will."

And we're out of a job, anchors away. Swift, elegant waters cutting into old shorelines, modes of consciousness. Arms, hands unlocked. A little closer to salvation.

KING'S CROSS

At times the wind influences the heart before the mind can look back upon its thoughts and trace a course, apprehend an impact. Like a song sinking directly through the muscle of legs, feet, and toes. The realignment of grace.

So, the soul *does* need saving, and full embodiment to transmit its infinite gleam.

Thirty degrees centigrade. The late summer humidity works through each of our pores, in a sixth-floor room with a skylight set high across a sloping ceiling, and a ladder reaching against a white wall.

Ana climbs the ladder toward the skylight. A bedsheet enfolds her body as she climbs, and as she climbs she opens the bedsheet to the light and air there. I lie back on the bed, an eye on her loosened hair.

"If you lean out carefully you can see the cathedral in one direction and the ocean in the other," she says.

This she does, an acrobat, balanced upon a top rung, looking both ways.

"And at night you can bathe in starlight."

Her voice and accent defy the Russian landscape she once traversed. English slips from her tongue like a dare. English lifted from books, newspapers, cafés. A self-taught crash course practised before a host of mirrors, simple in tone.

She turns on the ladder, and props her back and legs against its rungs, poised as if in standing meditation. She looks up through the skylight. She opens the bedsheet and waves it like a cape, allowing fresh air to flow in and out. She shakes her dark hair, an auburn waterfall. She looks at me with such honesty, a smile suffused with the miles it has taken her to arrive here in this room. Like a runner breaking stride, slowing her pace, sinking feet into the earth.

"Why did you stop?" she asks.

"Stop?"

"Before," she says, "when we were *fucking*. You stopped."

She uses the word *fucking* without the weight and misfortune of the West, with all the clarity and surprise of someone who has just plucked a seashell from beneath a mound of tin cans.

"Why? Why did you stop?"

"Because," I say, "it's been a long time since I've been eye to eye like this."

She looks at me without challenge, curious, a new lover. Eager to unwrap character and wounds and wonder. Our mouths full of light and care.

She nods and waves the sheet. Her hair glimmers beneath the skylight, streams of light penetrating her auburn roots. The whiteness of her flesh comes through, like a beacon, undoing my eyes.

She tells me she worked for a ballet company. Not a dancer, just a stagehand, she says. A production assistant.

"You're kidding me, pulling my leg," I say, because of how her legs appear. Strong, agile; part trunk, part branch. Capable of a sudden leap, then sudden stillness.

There was nothing to her leaving the Soviet Union, or Mother Russia, as she calls it. She won't call her leaving a defection. Too dramatic, too serious. Heroic.

"The company was performing in Athens," she says. "One night I got up from my bed and wandered down to the hotel lounge. I was looking at a small globe of the world on a tabletop, and I wondered why I had been living as if the world were flat. I left the hotel and didn't return."

"That's it?"

"That's it," she says. "Now I'm here. Your embrace is the only boundary I desire."

She unravels the bedsheet from around her body and shoulders and leans away from the ladder, balanced. She tosses the heaped sheet over my body. When she looks at me I'm no longer worried about where I leave off and another begins. Then she jumps, a clean flight, landing beside me and rolling over. Her body is warm. Her breasts full and scented with the dried sweat of our earlier lovemaking. The imprint of her pulse travels across my chest.

"This time," she says, "don't stop."

The last of the evening light like lemon zest presses through the skylight. In this kind of heat there is only one way to relieve it: close our eyes and bring one another to orgasm with only our fingertips. When we open our eyes, the world has changed places with a new moon.

She keeps the walls of the room bare. She finds solace near my navel. She compares my belly to a well. She stirs it until the humidity thickens and turns to sweat. She drinks.

I claim the sole of her left foot. It holds the scent of a field this side of spring, a furrow worked and reworked, then left fallow. Each morning I check the foot, lend a moistened kiss, and wait.

We go shopping. This she loves, the simplicity of it, no Soviet lineups. With so much choice, and air, a modern crowd loses its urgency. There's no competition for the last can of peas or a slab of cheese. In the absence of real hunger, she says, she almost forgets to say thank you.

When she's showering I linger in bed. Naked. Doing nothing. We haven't even talked about the fact that I'm heading one way and she another. How long can we sustain ourselves like this? This mysterious waltz. Our embrace has become so close that just the slightest touch, a fingertip against her dark nipple, a tongue pressing against my testicle, moves us to cry out as if our whole lives depended on it. We're co-creating moments that stretch back as far as the body can remember, when the galaxies and swamps bathed in the same elemental origins. When we emerged from single cell beings.

When we lie back in bed, I almost forget myself to the point of remembering. Halfway around the world, or halfway back. I'm drunk with distance and timelessness, ashes, sands, oceans, and forest monasteries. There is a prayer in my heart I can't conceive of alone, a God not yet flesh. I carry this like seed, along with the dead, so small now. There is nothing hidden between us, not even the moods we assume to disguise our personal histories.

I open the medicine pouch and show Father's ashes to Ana, finger the soft remains. I tell her about Father's paintings, his love of forests and oranges. How his works were always set outdoors, a tabletop among the sugar maples. His love of white pine stumps, birch, great blackened trunks scarred by lightning. How every image was caught in an act of collapse or embrace, or entwined as both. How the table-tops sunk their legs like roots, into the Canadian Shield. I tell her how an empty canvas would haunt Father, bring him to tears, until he learned how to ask its permission to release its storm and story, its warm, living light.

Where joy is most potent, it is fed by the wisdom of grief.

Ana is sleeping. Against my body, creased like the white sheets, she is sleeping the sound sleep of a Sunday morning. Three a.m. I'm woken by a dream of bells. I slip out of bed, out from against Ana's light body, the warm wave of her hair. It doesn't matter where I go, how I move, her aroma is with me. She's in my blood now, like a perpetual offering. I think of Jesus healing the ten lepers and of them running off, delirious with new life. Only one of them returns to give thanks. Why do we make love? To be that one person returning, gratitude endowed with praise.

I climb the ladder. I poke my head through the open skylight, feel the night air. I can see the cathedral to the west, a bricked-in structure, under the harsh influence of nightlights. Each brick seems to waver, as if the entire cathedral is undergoing an interrogation. A captive now to thirst. If I had the shoulders and the strength and the legs and feet of a mythical hero, I'd take that cathedral for a walk, out into the dewy world. A hot and wet afternoon.

Mother took me to St. Michael's Cathedral in Toronto when I was young. Good Friday. I remember kissing Jesus's feet on the cross. Small, raw toes. The cold of the cross pressing against my lips terrified me. The painted crimson blood had no taste. Not a hint of earth.

Later there was Mother, on her knees at the foot of her bed, demanding mercy to relieve her depression. Beethoven's *Fifth Symphony* knock knocking through the house, breaking down doors.

I loosen a few of Father's ashes. Let them go from the opening in the skylight. I watch the ashes ripple on air toward the cathedral. An act of contrition without the accomplishment of wings.

Ana travels with a viola. Mornings she sits on a chair beneath the skylight, and with fingers and bow she plays notes of grace, notes of repose, notes of the liminal. She compares her own body to that of the viola, two naked instruments. She tells me not so much about *tuning* her viola but about bringing it into alignment with the beat of her heart so that both the harmonics of her body and the sounds educed from the viola might arise as a unified whole. Before playing she sits quietly, honing in on the spirit of her breath. The sacred is the note to which she tunes herself, she says. Now to make love unveils a truer state of play.

We cut into a pineapple. Share half-moon slivers. Pick rind from teeth. Chew until every ounce of juice has dripped like sap into our bellies. This too becomes part of our lovemaking. The waltz, the heated confluence of desire. Our bodies sift and mingle, shift like continental plates, then suddenly drop off into deeper waters, loose and humming. We become the music lifted from an incomplete manuscript, drifting upwards into the arms of a song about the sea.

"I won't hold you to anything," she says. "But the truth."

She has a scar above her right eyebrow. It was received from an empty glass thrown by her mother on the five-hundred-and-ninety-fifth day her father had been deprived of any meaningful work. Ana just happened to be in the way.

"That's how it is in a totalitarian state," she says. "You just happen to be in the way."

Her twenty-eight-year-old body is loosening its precious stone, the ancestral. Ripe, bold forms carved into her gestures. Animal and woman, subterranean spirits singing through the holy pores of her skin. There are wide, flickering rivers running the space between her breasts. A space where language is learned, purified, and blessed. Memory germinates here without the weight of sin. Her body, her damp breath, the salted muscles. We trust our nakedness with an eye toward a future when to make love is considered a subversive act. How else does the Word become flesh?

I touch her forehead, her full cheeks, her lips purpling from all our kissing. She talks of her mother's face, the proud and heavy expressions she wore. A face, Ana confides, like the backside of an old wooden door, with three hooks, and hanging from the hooks, heavy, weathered overcoats and old scarves knit and knit again, and hats with patches on them. Each year the door, the grain in the wood is painted over and over, black on brown into black. Each year it moves a little further away from the forest which first pressed it into being. Now I touch her shoulders, the quivering wing tips. She speaks of her father, fragile as a china bowl.

"I was afraid to hug him," she says, "for fear he'd break at my touch."

I touch her rib cage, the slim, wakeful curve of bone. She speaks of a brother, fourteen years her elder, broken off from the family. A real defector, he escaped the State before she could say his name. He wrote to the family, letters which always arrived opened and resealed. He wrote of the weather, of work, of overtime, but never mentioned his insides, the climate there. The letters once ceased, then suddenly began again, this time cleansed of the Russian language, this time in English as well, written from San Francisco, written like a man who had not only escaped his own country but his own body as well. Ana read and reread the letters, looking for clues. Looking for a way a new language might liberate her but keep her body intact.

I touch her chest, the solar plexus, the murmuration of her heartbeat coming through. I trace a finger along her belly, the inner fold of her labia, her trembling thighs. She whispers of a grandmother making love with a grandfather in a forest vale, two uncaged birds, clipped, but mammal in strength, stretching the last of their breaths toward one another, determined to perpetuate the human race when all around them the blasted soils cracked and bulged with Stalin's dead.

"My grandmother told me in secret that she couldn't put her back against the earth and make love without taking in the groans of the dead, without her flesh becoming parchment for their stories," Ana says.

She keeps a handwritten copy of Psalm twenty-two tucked away inside her soft leather viola case. Her grandmother passed the psalm onto her, a prayer that charges and surrenders at the same time. The tongue moves instinctively from rage to praise in a matter of lines.

Now I brush a place inside. Ana's eyes are closed. The world within is larger than how we see it with eyes opened. She hesitates to speak of this place, words stuttering. I have to piece this story together, gather fragments, the quick dabbing strokes of an Impressionist painting. I have to stand back to take in the whole.

In this place of memory, there's a lover, a young man and a third growing in her womb, in a far Soviet city. Nine months and two heartbeats inside her. Then the twenty hours of labour and her silent howls linked with each breath. "The cramping," she says. When she saw the nurse's eyes become moist and the doctor turning his head, she knew something was wrong. The babe too silent to know a first breath. And her lover then slipping off the hospital gown, slipping through the white doors. Nineteen years old and shocked in love and loss.

She rolls over, gasping. There is something unanswered opening in her strong bones, her shoulders a narrow ridge. She asks me to massage her feet. She speaks of the soles of the feet as an old cruciform cathedral entrance where God gets in and out.

She finds the tight skin along my left arm where I was burned, the damp fuse there like a line running through my body, down into my belly, down through my legs, my right foot alternating between air and nothing. I no longer disobey the ancient command to love.

We pull the bed into the centre of the room and place it beneath the open skylight, attracted to the first rain in weeks. Rain drops slip through the skylight, dollops thick as honey. The storm is quick and warm, flashing blue and grey. We don't move until the rain has stopped, until it is humid again and the rain has mingled with our sweat. We share in a single well system now, lifting waters through our cloudless hands.

She's wrapped a pocket-sized map of the world around a tennis ball. A small globe in the centre of the bed. She rubs her fingers across Canada, curious about what it harbours within its curves and depths, its social and cultural landscapes.

"Is it like your body?" she asks, leaning into my arms, her hair smelling of salt and rain.

I try to fill in the landscape for her, to honour the spaces I would hardly recognize anymore. The chinook winds, the Prairies' fragile skin, living and dying in the hold of grain and frost. The warm lakes of July, a deep inhaling light, followed by autumn shedding its summer flesh. Then the freeze again and the sound of skates and hockey pucks sliding over ice, bodies arching, undone by snow and three layers of sweat. I speak of a land bound by intricate neighbourhoods and fantastic spaces, glacial ravines, its people threading worlds. The many tapestries and creeds and recipes carried with them from around the planet; the backdoor religions, the dining-table conversations, the bedrooms and last rites. It's a land as fragrant and tempered and tragic as anywhere, I say. Ana places a finger to my lips, an ear against my chest. We are as distinct as we are enfolded with one another.

The last of the moon pulling through the skylight, pulling on distant tides. There is the sweet aroma of far-off orchards swaying with the coming of winter, getting into the room. Everything about our embrace is shaped by the solitude of the other's story. Words add humus to touch. So that something not yet known, flesh or not, named or not, might take root and ignite its voice within.

This is not what I expected. To travel so far, to lose so much, to lie with my face on another woman's belly, Ana's, and wonder about the first sound that flared out over creation. That such a sound and song might emerge from so fragile and firm a belly.

We stay awake between three and four in the morning. A vigil. Certain that it is our prayers that at this moment gives the night its ineffable radiance. When we sleep it is because we trust other lovers are up, keeping vigil in their chosen rooms, all around the world, keeping vigil so that the radiance of a thousand lovers keeps spreading. It's the radiance that map-makers follow, use to mark their way. Roads, pathways, old pilgrim routes east and west, the Milky Way alighting the way.

Ana is sitting up in bed. The tennis-ball map of the world, which has been sitting on top of the dresser, rolls over, drops to the floor, and bounces across the room. A third hand moving things, unexplained. I place my head upon her quiet belly. The path to our becoming is accompanied by so many aches and ancestral plungings. There is always the ascending and descending work, the flux within.

Ana begins to speak in circles. How we travel. The direction she has been seeking, the direction my body has pursued. How we've intersected and the methods of our arrival. An affirmation of kiss. She speaks of risking ourselves to open spaces.

"So few trust in the gravitational pull of their love," she says, "when all along allurement is the very nature of the Universe."

She is preparing us to leave, her voice drawing the road. She's heading toward a New World, San Francisco, a brother she longs to know. I feel the tug of the Old World, its philosophical landscapes. Ana insists she will find me, like a psalm line finds the cracks in a stained glass window, filling the sky. She gives me the address of a hotel in Athens.

"If you happen to pass through. Room seven is nice."

I wrap a portion of Father's ashes in a fragment of the blue tissue paper I received from the young man in Fiji. I fold the tissue in two, then place the wrapping inside Ana's viola case, next to the handwritten psalm.

"I've left behind a path of ashes," I say. "If you happen to get lost."

She cuts a circular piece of Russia from her map, a section of Leningrad hugging the Gulf of Finland. She draws a small figure of a fish, like the fish the early Christians drew on their catacomb walls, over the gulf waters.

"I used to swim in those waters until my body ached for freedom," she says.

The ocean wind, through the skylight, lifts the bedsheet. Two bodies unmoored. We agree whenever possible we will wake at 3 a.m. and put on the night skies.

Our vigil hour.

When the imaginal roads and the great physical roads of the world converge and wed, perhaps then we learn to see with complete eyes; and the transcendent world pierces the immanent world of earth and bone, the lives and deaths and lovers each of our bodies contains.

IN FLIGHT

Grounded in Darwin, Australia's Northern Territory. A wide ribbon of unyielding globe, a world unknown.

I have a twenty-four-hour layover. Must be thirty-six degrees Celsius.

Not an easy landing here. The plane experiences engine trouble thousands of metres over the Tanami Desert. The night skies are so clear, and so close to the counter-glow of the sun, that sands glitter below.

When the body achieves the cold-blooded heights, the ecology of the mind becomes almost ethereal. Ley lines show through the skin, activate the eternal.

About the engine trouble the pilot announces, "Not to worry."

I don't understand the mechanical world, what keeps us up. Engines and their combustive groans, sometimes a hum and a bump. To ease the uncertainty about a metal craft solely hooked on speed, I imagine Father's red canoe, the two of us on one of our journeys into Algonquin Park, dipping paddles, pulling back, steering with the ingenuity of a J-stroke. The sun and moon doing the important work, influencing us ashore.

Not to worry.

I grip Father's ashes in my left hand, like prayer beads. Like sleeping bells dreaming through the last seconds before the celebration of midnight Mass.

There must be one hundred of us on board, powering over the slow and sober horizon. Not to worry. And for a minute, more, the engines cut out, lose power. We're orbiting in retrograde motion. Gliding, drifting, silent in our descent. I imagine the grace of the red canoe over still waters. Then I struggle for my hold. I notice the man and woman next to me, hands, fingers interlocking.

So high above the ground, slanting now. I see it is my longing that casts itself down, my body having to forgive gravity. I was never in control. Not even when I had the steering wheel in my hands, my foot tense, alternating between brake and gas pedal.

I see the landscape below, packed tight as a bud. Everything slowing. I see tender soils stirring in their earthen vase, faint hillsides coming into view and mounds of stone ruminating with a rapture so pure and unattached, my fears release. This is a land shaped by billion-year-old constellations, lying dormant just beneath the earth's crust. An energy trembling beneath layers translucent as waves. All this I see suddenly rising up into the starlit world, enfolding the plane. Pressed between altitude and diminishment, when death holds itself as revelation, we surrender into the unspeakable name of God.

Not to worry.

And the engines kick back in, one hundred of us exhale. We lift our eyes, our breaths on loan. The man and the woman next to me, eyes wide, look at me as if we've known one another a very long time.

Darwin's heat is impossible to escape. A blind, sinking heat. It gets into the skin's every aspect, curls the hair, and conquers the voice. It is cruel and irreversible. In such heat, memories and musings and any sense of separation, seem laughable. Deeply laughable.

Laughing rouses the soul.

There are a few cultures and languages that don't have the word *loneliness* in their vocabulary. I wander the streets of sticky Darwin, sharpened by the heat. I settle in a cut of shade on a bench next to a small Bible chapel. Two young missionaries speak with a man on the street by the chapel. The missionaries talk about God and the Good News and of all things, loneliness. Two young men, Bibles in hand and hair groomed for the air force, speak of the human soul as a lonely, isolated thing, a terrible thing in need of saving, a scorched thing, lonely for God. The man stands still, listening. Unhooked, it seems, from the need to be hooked. A well-toned man with braided black hair and a face that seems pressed with the dark landscape I've just flown over, he begins to examine his body, his hands, their palms, his arms up to the elbows, as if his body were a dictionary and he was searching for a meaning. The man then shifts his stance, and asks the missionaries about this word *loneliness*, this terrible thing which makes you lonely for God. Where does it come from, this animal-like thing, this loneliness out to get him? The missionaries rally, flip through their Bibles, and say something about the feeling of being unbearably alone in an overcrowded world, a world soaked in sin.

The man turns and looks out over the street and the lands and the horizon beyond, then asks the missionaries if they were not at home with the sun and the moon, the rivers and hills and valleys, and all things visible and invisible which travel within and between two bodies?

"This is the Living Book," the man then says, gesturing with his hand across the landscape. "The first one of its kind."

And he wanders off, face to the setting sun.

I spend the evening out of the heat, remaining on the bench. Still and quiet, all sky. Planes, Bibles, chapels. *Don't confuse the cup for the taste*, I think. A janitor shows up around ten o'clock to clean the chapel. When he locks up, he passes me by, nodding my way, G-night.

When it seems the night is at its thickest pitch I release a few of Father's ashes, flashing like fireflies against the chapel doors. I don't know if there's anything more lonely than a place of worship under lock and key.

I skip now like a smoothed stone over air currents and waters: the Arafura Sea, the Flores Sea, the Java Sea. Three, four, five skips. A heartbeat in ripple motion over a low, wide world. Horizons which teach my arms about embracing lands I have not yet walked. Memory stripped down to the essentials, the simple beauty of being.

Toward Singapore. The DC-3 banks over Borneo, a small detour, out of the way of major flight paths. The pilot wants to show us something. The sea below turns blood-black and green, and rises toward us, like a thousand hands holding up strange baskets full of light. Then I realize it isn't the sea at all but a rainforest, leaves gesturing, tipping the whole forest canopy toward its apogee. My eyes tear, my hands fall open. I see it all, the whole of the forest, wet and silent, its intense summits formed by feral branches and bright bark. So many secret lives beneath its succulent leaves, unmapped. The man sitting next to me, a man named Ravi, a teacher of religious studies at an English school in Western Samoa, tells me the main survival concern for those who inhabit the forest below us is not disease, or fierce, poisonous creatures, or multinational logging companies annexing a way of life, but of falling limbs, great branches shedding themselves and crashing down through everything in their path. Ravi says the people down there in the rainforest have learned to walk with one eye on the ground and the other looking up through the trees. They walk slowly, an ear alert to what falls.

Ravi introduces me to Singapore's heat. A thick, surrendering equator-bound heat. A heat that does not inspire the body to lose itself in lovemaking. That kind of heat belongs to another sun.

Ravi is on his way to Madras, and from there to an ashram outside the city where his first teacher lives and prays like a man who has rolled away every obstacle from his door.

"My teacher is dying," Ravi says. "I must see him before his dies and give my thanks. A man most becomes himself at death."

The man is his father.

I imagine that if the world's bodies of water could form sound into human speech, they would sound like Ravi's voice. A subtle roll beneath which the spray of a wave rises up like the breath of a newborn, faint on a mother's lips.

We sit in a second-floor curry house, and eat our food from banana leaves, using our hands. We searched for hours for such a place, Ravi stepping carefully, evenly, hands folded near his chest, eyes wide, his whole body tuning in to just the right spice wavering in the doorway of just the right restaurant. The proprietor stands nearby, smiling, graceful, hands behind his back, happy to witness so many people enjoying his food. There's a spice in the dish that sends sweat in a swirl over our foreheads.

"Keep breathing," Ravi says. "Eating a good curry is as close as food gets to the purification of the body."

Being with Ravi is like encountering a fifth season dawning over the world. He's interested in Father's ashes. Why do I carry them? To what end?

"There's a place in Spain," I offer, "Finisterre, where the ancients believed the world came to an end, fell away. Father sometimes wondered about such a place when we studied maps. What it must be like to confront your cultural and political limitations, a world view pushed back by an ocean."

Ravi nods, looking me in the eye.

"For now I just want to honour him," I say. "His memory. His work. His hands."

We have twelve hours together before Ravi's flight leaves for Madras. We make a pact not to sleep: we'll walk the night streets, let what happens happen. "The way of the spirit," Ravi says, giving ourselves over to the freshness of each step.

Whenever we meet up with someone he thinks he knows, or with a stranger just met for the first time, he gives a little bow while placing his hands together in a reverent manner, then opens his hands outward to the person and bows again. "A gesture meant to welcome what is divine in the other," he says.

We find a bench in a small square where the trees are overly pruned, leaves pulled tight. At one end of the square is a church, Catholic, I think. A wedding is just letting out. People filter down the stairs, fresh and elegant. The wedding couple appears, a festival of cheers over their heads, amidst dusk and the heat. Next door there's another church, or a temple, Buddhist, Ravi says, and another wedding is letting out. The two wedding parties intermingle and exchange their peace.

At the other end of the square is a group of garbed men crowding around an open door. The men huddle, raise their voices, hands and fingers wagging, as if bartering, flashing money. Two women, one in red, the other in black, stroll between the men. They angle their bodies back toward the open door. The bartering doesn't seem to hold the women's attention. They turn slow, defiant steps, waiting, sure of themselves. The men become anxious, hurried, on the brink of economic collapse. The woman in black leaves the crowd of men, the open door at her back. She begins a measured walk across the square, beneath the tightened leaves. Her walk is part schooled, part street, all money and rose-red lips. When she stands before us, she places her hands on her hips. Ravi bows to her, opening out his hands.

"*Namaste*," he says.

"If you say so," the woman in black says, a half-cheek grin.

She hones in on Ravi, as if on a kindred spirit.

"Do I know you?" she asks. She has the voice of a room where the bedsheets have been pulled back.

"While you were walking over here a thousand temptations to know you crossed my mind," Ravi says.

"Temptation is a gift of the Goddess Rati," the woman in black says. "I promise not to tell your wife."

"She already knows." Ravi smiles, and gestures toward me. "She's in his heart, listening."

The woman in black flashes her red, red lips.

"Birds," she says. "Two odd birds."

She turns her hips and shoulders away, moves into the square toward the open door across the way. How many lives are layered in that walk? How many of us strangers and our incomplete dreams? Is it easier to find sanctuary in those we don't know rather than within the complex layers of someone loved and named?

The heat loosens its grip, lifting as midnight nears. Diesel fumes and exotic scents compete and fill the air. To sit so quietly with a man on a bench: a calm comes over me as dew over a river valley, so moist you can wash yourself down with the soaking leaves. Ravi and I take off our shoes. He's the same age as Father would be. Ravi's father has reached the age I imagined Father would achieve had he been allowed to grow slowly into death, into that darkness unobserved by dawn.

Three in the morning. I remember the promise with Ana. I send my love prayers above the city, back across the flight paths I have travelled, rippling above the treeline. Where language fails, let the Universe articulate what it is I cannot say. Supernovas, black holes, two stars in behind the mountains, making camp. My prayers follow the lantern lights cast by nomadic tents along a desert floor.

Ravi's voice drifts, eyes waning. He's speaking about rivers, about how his father escorted him to the Ganges when he was a boy of twelve. The rituals of burning the dead he witnessed, the colourful shrouds and the smell of sandalwood and mango offerings, and the chants of the mourners as they jogged round the fire. "God's name is truth," they sang. Now, thinking of his father dying, a body changing form, he questions the scar of grief that will come. He imagines his wife's upper arms, the thick flesh there where he has found rest for his head when overcome. Then he quotes from a holy book, the Bhagavad-Gita. The young warrior Arjuna has come face to face with an *enemy* comprised of his kinsmen and friends. Struck by the absurdity of having to battle loved ones, Arjuna says: "My limbs sink down, and my mouth becomes parched, and there is a trembling in my body, and my hair stands on end. The bow falls from my hand, and my skin, too, is burning, and I cannot stand still, and my mind seems to wander."

"Revelation is a thirst," Ravi says. "As long as we have an enemy, we are the enemy. Grief need not be feared. We're only as wise as our wounds."

He leans his head back against the bench, edging my left shoulder, the smell of coriander on his breath.

"I need a little rest," he says.

When my mother was claimed by death, Father and I sat in the hospital corridor waiting for the morticians to arrive. It was three fifteen in the morning, a long day in April. I felt myself slipping, as a body in an icon of the Resurrection, turned upside down, falling back into the black earth. I fell against Father's shoulder, wanting his pulse, wanting sleep. If I slept it would all go away. Mother's passing, the cancer, her depression; gone. But sleep only raised what I most feared, a dream of Mother up and walking, watering flowerpots on a windowsill. When Father eased me awake, a hand through my hair, I thought I had been asleep for hours. I looked to the clock in the hospital corridor. 3:25 a.m.

I sense a chill at my back, something moist. One, two, maybe three drops of rain. By the time I look up, the only cloud has passed. A pale morning star floats into view. A new heat arrives with dawn. My feet are angled and naked against the cold concrete. I daydream about white pine roots, lichen on bark.

A ladybug flickers across the bench, across Ravi's thighs, bright orange against his white linen pants. The ladybug climbs Ravi's finger and settles into his upturned palm, finds the lifeline there. I lay my hand down next to Ravi's. The ladybug flutters, makes the leap, and lands in the palm of my hand. I can see the sun sudden and flaring in the ladybug's orange shell.

Who is this self that suffers? I remember asking myself. I imagine if the sun were to run around the Universe in search of the source of its light, in a constant state of having forgotten the self-illuminating nature of its being, that would be a life of suffering.

Ravi must go. It's a few hours until his flight. He asks a gift of me before I can think of what to offer: to have a pinch of Father's ashes. To carry them to his country, the ashram, his own father's bedside. So that when his father's body is burned on its funeral pyre and afterwards deposited as ashes in the Bay of Bengal, he might include my father's ashes, as if to supply the loving energy an experienced soul can offer, to help release what the body has long been in preparation for.

"If we are joined in the ancestral realm, which I believe we are," Ravi says, "then it is essential we become good ancestors now. Buoyed by the thousand lives that hold us up."

Ravi kisses me on both cheeks, the tickle of his beard in our exchange of peace. When he's gone, the bus passing through the street, I rub the place on my cheek, rub awake his scent of coriander.

A soft breeze touches down upon the waking streets. I imagine spinning the compass as Father spun the globe on his desk, spinning a roulette wheel. It takes all my humility not to stop the spin. Let wonder harness the orbit, the trajectory of scientists, philosophers, and saints.

With each flight I imagine holy people, Moses, Jesus, going up into their mountains and waiting on their God, their hearts like fresh tablets, part stone, part wood; the word of God coming through. The mountain air is blazing and drunk, circulates the world like an old song.

Singapore to Athens. The headlines say Saddam Hussein's army has invaded Kuwait. All the winds of the world are now heading for that desert where a singular line cuts Kuwait and Iraq in two. Into this greying and humid and rocking world we ascend. A long flight becomes an affair of detours around the Middle East. Drinks are on the house. Three in-flight films are shown, the hot summer releases. I look out into the thick night sky, a black screen across which something alive flickers: Ana's afterglow.

So the plane slips over this holy land, navigating its many sites of war, wailing walls, and faith. I see the glimmer of valley worlds, ancient forests merging into desert roads. I see the Persian world, then Mecca and Jerusalem, in the mysterious distance of my mind. I'm surprised by so much green. All the desert stories I've read, the prophet's rants, the holy lands I've studied, seemed devoid of greening lives. Encounters with green being so rare and scarce, so powerful a vision, that they could only be the energies of God, burning to speak.

PILGRIM

Like Father's ashes. Like the wild planet, blue and green when seen from outer space. The earth in sacred spin, without maps, clear and distinct. Generous in her becoming.

ATHENA

Take a dusty elder grape between forefinger and thumb. Roll it gently, squeezing inward, and kneading the skin until the interior life of the grape gives and the juice breaks through. So the world of ancient light over Greece greets me.

Ana, now I know why you chose this city to leave your old life. Athens doesn't require undressing. It's already naked. For all its haze and pollution and humidity, it's a city that doesn't rush or beg to please me. It rises, patiently, like a god's foot from a footstool. It's a city influenced by blue, a cut jewel. It sets in behind my eyes before I have a chance to look away. The blue of its light means to polish my every breath and pulse. My body becomes like smooth marble as the summer air presses into my flesh. Everything from my skullcap to my belly to my feet, to how I view the world of art and religion and the wind, is realigned. If the blue of Athen's light and heat doesn't cleanse me, then the white mountains and hills will offer their means of conversion. How I step through an open door is changed. There is a blessed relationship between the growing lines beneath my eyes and the rings in a table-top's wood or the wood of great altars. My sweat becomes the stuff of myth and passage. I slow before the trembling red of an icon whose paint is still damp.

Athens is a city so ancient, it has come around on itself again. It has no need of time. As if the Universe were still working itself out here. As if the Big Bang theory was first tested here, flared out, the world forever blossoming in the flower boxes of an Athenian windowsill.

I find the hotel just off Omonia, the one Ana recommended. Room seven is occupied but five is just as nice, bright and potent. "There's a letter here for you, sir, we've been holding it for a week or so."

> *Love, I think I see you in each passing face.*
> *There's water in my dreams. San Francisco*
> *hums in my ear like your voice, painted*
> *flowers, circles. I dream of our room, a kiss,*
> *the new year of our love. In the gathering of*
> *desire, your Toronto, my heart. A.*

To appreciate the streets and the people and the gleam of an Athenian world view, Ana said I must at times stop and stand on my head and leave my unanswered prayers for a new posture, a new way of seeing. Athens doesn't mean to solve life's mystery but to bring you into a shapelier balance with the cosmos, she said. Athens teaches you to flow, to meander. So I find myself just walking. Any other means of transportation would be to miss the mark. I find myself walking south from Omonia, pulled by blue, by the aroma of fresh coffee, of more diesel, of leather, of wool flokati rugs, of second-hand bookstores. I step into the Monastiraki flea market, I come upon junk polished anew, copper and brass icons, depicting the faith of a thousand years, more. Then into the northern shade of the Acropolis I turn, into the Plaka; no cars. Here life seems divested of outside dramas. The hillsides and mountains have come down for a visit and nestle into the arms of men and women and children. What is shared here is not so much the food but the view, the unlimited stretch of the human heart. This is a country that does not struggle with identity. That's what a café owner tells me, a young man named Neilos. Noticing that for three or four days straight, a few hours each morning and a few hours each night, I don't move from my table, he feels compelled to share his view.

Neilos has travelled Mexico, the States, Canada. He knows about life on Toronto's Danforth, GreekTown. Then he shocked his system and found himself in the heart of Africa, Zambia. "As a child my father would talk about God," Neilos shares, "and my mother would pray to God," he says, "but in Zambia, in Zambia I found citizens who danced as God." He savoured that dance, and danced himself, while recognizing in the dance the shape of a woman he loved. So he returned to Athens, his beloved city, his beloved Diana.

Our third night together, Neilos's young wife, Diana, and their first-born daughter, Apphia, join us. It is the beginning of their holidays, a month of feasts. Diana, with hair prepared, conditioned by a morning swim in the sea, Apphia chewing on first sounds; *baba* for bread, for mother's fingers, each breast full. During feeding, Neilos conducts the night at dusk in the Plaka; the beat of conversations and music from a radio; the clatter of footsteps and cutlery against plates. The mystery of unlit lanes.

A sweet, cool white wine cradles my tongue, now a revived instrument. Goat cheese and thick bread, black olives, accompany each sip.

Neilos holds his face and head up to the night light. A handsome, rigorous face. The beginning of soft creases fanning out beneath his deep, brown eyes.

"Think about it," he whispers. "What makes this spot so rich? Why are we here? Because it started here, right? This grand thing we call the Western experiment. Not just the gods and goddesses come down to show us how to play through our loves and sorrows, no. But this slow burn and dance we call democracy. This fragile bird-of-process we hold in hand. Think of it, only a handful of civilizations have tried it and most have failed, right? Most of humanity has endured nothing but tyrants and fat monarchs and warlords. But what did that great American say, 'a government of the people, by the people, for the people.' Think of the responsibility that is required of every single one of us to be involved in that kind of governance system. Think of the forever vigilance that is needed. Yes. What we celebrate here is this crazy idea called democracy. This tender tool we often take for granted. How these star-seeds above us and these hearts and minds within us even imagined something as wild as democracy, it stills the mind."

Diana sits forward, smiling, holding Apphia while placing a finger upon her husband's lower lip, and says, "Stills the mind, indeed."

Neilos's smile breaks across the Plaka. He looks to his wife and daughter with deep love and care. We sit, silenced then, sparkling a little like embers banked against the shadows of the Acropolis.

Then Diana hands me her daughter. I cannot describe the gesture: Was it designed by a divine aspect? The wind? A dream?

I sit back, holding Apphia in my arms. I feel the calm of her sleep against my chest. I can smell her sweet, milky breath. If the world were to end, if its fascination with itself, if its many threats of war were to erupt, Athens would remain, the Plaka intact, a little bruised but blazing like an eye looking out over a far sea. Athens has undergone eons of deforestation and desertification to the point that it can find itself again replanted at a café table, exchanging in the eternal of an idea. Time bends an ear.

We ease through the evening. More wine, a seafood platter round midnight, salad and small roasted potatoes, a bowl of grapes. Athens is cooling. Between two and three in the morning, silence takes its place at the tabletop. Neilos rests with his head back against the white wall, slipping into the rest required of a man who is happy to just sit with the stars. Diana has Apphia back in her arms, feeding time again. In their quiet exchange of suckle and flow I sense the four elements undulating, enfolding us. We are travellers in our variant ways. We come to tabletops that inspire epic poems, epic journeys that articulate epic visions of the heart. We contain stories and paintings from the ages, depicting times and places when words are still fresh, newborn, and not bent on proving belief. When articles of faith are exchanged with a nod. As simple as the skin of a grape revealing the underbelly of the cosmos.

Ana, my mouth is sore with missing you.

Walking back to the hotel off Omonia, I realize I'm drunk. For the first time in years. Drunk. Drunk without thinking about Father's ashes, what to do. For a full night and day, for four or five days now, I have misplaced the intent of Father's ashes. All along I believed I could free myself of his death, Elle's death, of the unbearable shame, could save the situation from the hold of black ice, by slowly releasing Father's ashes over the earth. Now I see I'm drunk, disentangled from Father's ashes, and strangely no closer to liberation than I was at the time of the collision.

To Father, a map was like moist clay, like a lover's body, open to wanderlust. A curiosity for the details of another's landscape brings with it wonder and awe. Every step is a drop of water anointing the way.

The Port of Piraeus. I stand on the quay, eyes hooked on the Greek ships, their hulls brushing shoulders and hips, packed close like neighbours at a Saturday morning market. People everywhere are rushing with luggage and packsacks, bags overflowing with food, rushing to catch their ship to the islands. The blue of the water is so blue, my eyes fall to their knees. The Aegean is shrouded in a thick white haze, so thick it appears as a large bowl set upside down, the sun sitting on its back. The sun's light is diffused, slipping down the sides of the bowl, testing the waters. It soaks my mind. The humidity here moves through me like a ghost.

As the ship departs for the islands, the distinction between the Aegean heat and the heat of my flesh cracks open. My eyes find relief in the soaking shade of the third deck. Everyone wears white. The mainland drifts into the background.

Why does the language of grief have so many forms and rhythms? Why jazz, blues, slow rock ballads? How is it the Jew's harp and the zither bring about improbable arrangements? How is it the moon can plant itself at the foot of a sad song and linger for days? My flesh has become as papyrus upon which the Universe writes its music. As we approach the island of Siros, I sense a world of waves pulling me closer, calling me.

Siros. Legend has it Siros's first citizen, Coeranus, arrived on the island on a dolphin. He took refuge in a cave, in the lower hills, restoring his flesh in the blackness of earth's core. Homer gives mention to the island, a stopover for Odysseus. I stop here because I feel myself plucked. Plucked like figs and grapes from vines, fig trees. It's the island's two rooted peaks that also attract me, and the two churches up there, one Catholic, the other Orthodox. How they gaze into one another's open doors, from one peak to the other, like an old married couple renewing their vows. Within the slopes of San Tzortzis, inside the vestment of Ano Siros, I begin my climb, up through its narrow streets, its pebbled steps. Houses are dressed for Sunday. Blue sky everywhere. Such narrow streets, always going up into the sky. I become a little bit dizzy. Each step and bend straightens out, and each straightening becomes another step and bend. The Church of Saint George sits like a fossil atop the peak of

Ano Siros. Light seems to spill upward, a fresh, sweeping light lifted from the sea.

Mass is just beginning. The church doors are wide open. There are about twenty people present. A hint of incense in the air. The celebrant—a priest I come to know as Father Marcos SJ—is going through his many tongues, asking in Greek, German, French, Spanish, Japanese, English, Latin, if there is anyone who wishes to share in the daily readings and read aloud in their mother tongue.

I didn't expect my hand to react. My left arm, with its scarred layers folding and unfolding, shoots up. I must have appeared as a child in grade school, confident that I knew the answer to a difficult question. Father Marcos nods in my direction and in the direction of the pew across from me where a woman has raised her arm. The two of us stand and make our way to the altar, through the morning light now filling the church. Father Marcos scrutinizes us both as if he were an art dealer looking over a young artist's series of canvases.

"English," he says to me.

I nod.

"*Française*," he says to the woman.

"*Oui*," she says.

Father Marcos explains to us—in English, in French—how the Mass will work, its pure Latin sway. He'll nod to us when we are to read. Then he hands us the readings. I decide not to study my lines until the moment arrives when I am called, wanting the simplicity of the moment to ring with each word. Hoping that the sea-light that has accompanied my climb will amplify itself through my mouth and voice, clearing the nerves that pinch my throat.

"*In nomine Patris, et Fili, et Spiritus Sancti,*" Father Marcos intones.

Something catches hold of the church doors, slamming them shut. The light is caught inside like a moth. Everyone sits up, startled. Even Father Marcos breaks mid-prayer and looks back over his shoulder, his hands pressed against the altar. It is then I realize he is celebrating Mass in the old way, with his back to the congregation. I think of when Father took me to experience Miles Davis in concert, Massy Hall. Davis playing with his back to the audience. What mysterious source were his hands and breath tapping into?

"*. . . Christe, eleison . . .*"

I look back over my shoulder to see who might have slammed the doors shut. No one is there but the wind. A small woman, hair netted white, steps toward the doors and opens them again. The light and air move back in and out, unidentified scents join our prayers.

"*. . . Gloria in excelsis Deo et in terra pas hominids bone voluntatis . . .*"

History imprints sound. I imagine that veterans of war, like my grandfather, often cringe at the sound of a boot over cobblestone, a siren bludgeoning the night, or a door slamming in the distance. But what is the sound of a hand making a fist? Is there time to run? Mother's hands were like magician's hands, always pulling something from beneath her sleeveless summer dresses, her many-coloured bracelets. Candies, books, small shining gems. She seemed pressured to please, or was it a way of love? She never knew what door she'd cross through next: the door onto a summer stock theatre in Guelph, Stirling, or Stratford, or through a medical institution's doors on Queen Street. Her hands were a combination of attractive bowl, water-filled and swimming with flower petals; and a metal detector moving up and down her own body, checking for moods, their swings and uncoupled latches. Once, just once, when I talked back at her for being away so much, the hands seemed to lose themselves, flashing like an electric current, sweeping down the hallway then finding my right cheek, the side of my head and ear. I'd never felt something so physical go right through my body, levelling me. I lay on the floor, stretched out, unable to breathe. Afraid to cry or speak out, eyes staggering in the dark.

"... *Domine, Fili unigente, Iesu Christe, Domine Deus, Agnus Dei, Filius Patris, qui tollis peccata mundi, miserere nobis* ..."

Mother stood over me. It was futile to ignore what had just happened. Impossible to rearrange the walls, the light. The electric impulse of her hand. The future of sound had been altered. Mother's eyes began to swell. She recognized in my child's face her own desolation, cheekbones quivering. I saw her rib cage expand in the very place where my body had been cut loose from hers. Place of original blessing, place of secondary scarring. The cusp.

Father Marcos nods in my direction. I move toward the lectern. I can hear the wind at the doors again, then the stillness. I look to the reading, one I know by heart. Matthew. The sixteenth chapter. Lines twenty-four to twenty-six.

"For what profit is it to a man if he gains the whole world, and loses his own soul?"

It is not enough to say a woman looks beautiful in a particular dress. Father always said poetry recognizes it is the woman who makes the dress look beautiful. I give some of Father's ashes to the shoreline along the blue Aegean. Father's ashes not only look good in blue, they make the Aegean that more beautiful.

It has been a good week. The simple elation of a man who now sees he will not outlast the energy of the sun, or the supernovas of his dreams. Even a handsome object, like a Greek urn, or the many bracelets like spinning moons along Mother's arms, if cared for, will outlast my body; Mother's hands, Father's ashes.

I'm in the embrace of a strange new opening, received now through the mystery and landscape of an immense host.

PAX ROMANA

I'm walking now, the Old World and its ancient gleam. It's been a week of open roads and warm winds, the sun in Assisi's foothills like a saint. The eyes of his woods always look at me, every angle of my being.

It's been a few weeks since leaving Greece. I joined Father Marcos on a drive to Rome. The August holidays were drawing to a close, he was returning his nephew, George, and George's young wife, Sonia, to their home in Rome. Father Marcos makes this three-day pilgrimage by car each year, each year he says he moves a little closer to understanding what this holy city means to him.

"Rome is like a mistress," he said. "Though I have little idea what it's like having a mistress, you see."

I half expected him to wink, his tone suggesting he knew all about a life with a mistress. But it was the many confessions he had listened to, of men and their mistresses, of women and their lovers, that had influenced his tongue, how he saw the holy city, how his own soul flirted with his eyes, his mind.

We drove for hours, rolling over the Italian hillsides and mountains, the land soaked in a light that had been worked down into matter. We became faint with so much looking, looking and perspiring. To ease the view we drank lots of water, passed large sweating bottles around, and we chewed slowly on black olives, extracting their moisture, their black juice. The trees in places looked weather-worn, awkward, bent like an antiquated word—words like sacrifice, humility, reverence—that had lost its lustre.

There is a tendency when nearing a destination to speed up, lean into the wheel, will the car on, as if the destination itself draws us into its vortex. But Father Marcos adopted the opposite approach. He slowed down the car, faster vehicles honking horns at our rear, or pulled the car over to the side of the road so that we could observe our destination in the shimmering distance, a meditative honing in on the places where we would eat and sleep and be replenished.

Father Marcos didn't say anything. He sat at the wheel, hands in his lap. His eyes had the washed-over effect of two beach stones. It was impossible to feel impatient in his presence. I suppose he has studied these views a hundred times, each time he's made this pilgrimage to Rome. But his eyes, his demeanour, had that refreshed quality of seeing a place for the first time. I thought of a father receiving his firstborn child from the hands of the mother, and how he might present the child to the whole of the Universe. *This is my beloved son or daughter . . .*

The Italian hillsides, the curving and sweeping roads, are dotted with small, ornate crosses plunged deep into roadside shoulders, hammered into rock. Each cross marks time and place; marks an automobile accident, life, death, the in-between. Usually the crosses are at angled curves,

curves that slide dangerously round a blind bend, nothing but gnarled trees and scrub brush and rock face to guide us. Every curve was a dare and a grace. Every curve caused my body to tense in the back seat, my right foot feeling for a brake that wasn't there.

"You don't like cars, do you?" George said.

Sonia looked back over her shoulder. Her eyes told me what she saw, my face gone white. Father Marcos was at the wheel, negotiating each bend, sometimes with an eye in the rear-view mirror. He knew about Father's ashes, the collision that had altered our lives. Every cell in my body was busy visiting itself again, like an old man returning to his childhood neighbourhood, the house wherein he was born; sacred ground.

Father Marcos pulled the small red Fiat over onto a thin strip of land laced between two boulders. We were high in the Abruzzi hills, a slender piece of earth speckled with clear rock face and a light that seemed to breathe a blue heat. The road curved between two crosses bent into the ground. Both crosses were twisted and desolate, like an abandoned lover's limbs.

Time does not heal. It marks what has been lost, then wanders like a fugitive in its own land. Time is the death of wonder. A necessary tool but not a sufficient measure for grief. Grief desires space. A calming landscape where those we have lost work their way back to the surface of our skin and become the stuff of a scarred over wound. Grief is a sanctuary for truth. A crinkly map and we find ourselves setting out again toward places we thought we already knew and understood.

"I think we should celebrate this curve," Father Marcos said, his eyes leaving the rear-view mirror.

We got out of the car, into the open air. My bones tingled where they had once been broken. Father Marcos set a small green cloth across the trunk of the red Fiat, smoothing the cloth with both hands. Sonia had the bread, four thick slabs. George had the wine, dark as roots.

Father Marcos offered this Mass for our parents, first teachers of the heart. He asked for us to keep an open path into the body that might draw on genealogy and the communion of saints. He prayed for the reconstituted life of a cell.

George and Sonia placed a wallet-sized photo from their wedding, Father Marcos an aged black-and-white photo of his parents, creased at the edges, somewhat faded, on the green cloth. Father Marcos had his father's mouth and jaw, his mother's brow and eyes; handsome. I placed a portion of Father's ashes across the trunk of the red Fiat, and a photograph of Mother, her hair free. A blonde storm.

I read from Matthew.

"The kingdom of Heaven is like a mustard seed which a man took and sowed in a field. It is the smallest of all the seeds, but when it has grown it is the biggest of shrubs and becomes a tree, so that the birds of the air can come and shelter in its branches."

How is it that the Word conspires with the body and works to set each bone straight? What is a cross placed at the side of a road but a celebration of two more roads intersecting. That of the horizontal and that of the vertical. A synthesis of heart and mind. How I receive anything is how I receive everything.

After receiving communion, the bread and wine, how supple my flesh felt. We drove off slowly, windows rolled down. We didn't stop until dusk.

Rome is a city of ordinary saints, would-be saints, and thieving saints. It has its bakers and cooks and priests and sisters, and its pickpockets. Everyone is ordained for something. Home to a ministry of prophets and holy fools. It's a city where a civilization's collapse is celebrated as a burning victory.

Its heat has two purposes. To drive you out of town, or to push you deeper into any one of a thousand churches, edifices of stone cooled by the centuries.

Walking from the Church of Jesus to Saint Peter's, I'm followed by a band of young children, their complexions dark, fingers closing in. There's a wind inside my chest which has been there for ages, blowing up dust. I stop. There must be ten children, ages thirteen through four. Ten children and the illusion of one hundred hands, begging, pulling, and pushing at me. I sense a hand in my back pocket, another hand tugging at my shirt, another hand with a newspaper lifting over my packsack which is hanging over my left shoulder. Beneath the newspaper—dry headlines about Kuwait, Desert Shield, the promise of attack—is another hand, two hands, working at a packsack zipper into a compartment that I know is empty. Now there's no choice but to let my body sink to the ground, a cool church at my back. I sit squat, eye level with the children. One child with quickened brown eyes, quick and brown as water running a gutter system, looks at me, the look of a wall. I take the packsack off my shoulder, swing it around onto the ground before me. The one hundred hands stand back. There's only one thing to do. I open the packsack and show its contents. The one hundred hands lean in, and the boy with the brown eyes begins to fumble through the packsack, searching, each zipper leading into another layer of hunger. He finds the medicine pouch containing Father's ashes. He opens the pouch, stares, fingers the ashes, then lifts a speck toward his tongue, taking a taste. He squints, tightens his mouth, then spits the ash over the cobblestone road. When the boy with the brown eyes eases up his search and stands back, I see how far is his unrequited hunger from the cool darkness behind the church door. I realize there is a place in my body belonging to both of these worlds as well: the cool darkness and the hunger that feeds on ash.

The children leave with a few of my T-shirts, a shaving mirror, and a can of tuna.

The sin of not knowing what it is they really need, it is for this that I weep.

I am lost and ask a young man if I am on the right road to Saint Peter's. The young man takes me by the elbow and escorts me around a narrow corner, turns me round as if I am blindfolded in a game of pin the tail on the donkey, and, "Presto!" he says. Saint Peter's doors are right there before me, old growth remnants glinting a little, like a secret drawing me close. I don't know how long I spend inside, wandering. I find myself staring into the life of the *Pietà*, Mother Mary and a Son, her eyes circling back in on their source. Her quiet, mournful gaze. The stillness of death in her arms. Her gone Son. What's left but a taste of *repose* upon my tongue and an ache behind my knees. I enter the English confessional because the door there is open. And because I need to restore my mother tongue, reconcile my language, its ancient whisper. I'm responsible for the words I raise from my heart and give to the world. Then I find myself kneeling on the marble floor at Saint Joseph's altar. Mass. My heart's supple lament. Father, Elle. These years I've been shedding black ice.

I leave Rome on foot, walk through suburbs that remind me of why I left home

"Lord," Brother Francis sang, "make me an instrument of your peace."

Assisi flourishes in mutual relationship between its wildflowers and the stars. Both give off an undivided light that works to permeate the town's inner squares and streets. One breathes here and instantly feels the tender intimacy of the Universe.

The story of Francis: Exiled from father and mother and what was deemed as home. It seems his greatest blessing was in accepting banishment over the comforts of an inheritance. His inheritance was held over him as a threat, a manner of control, and not as a gift. Banishment became his suffering, suffering became his mentor. He lived a life of banishment within the streets and fields he regarded as home. He became a renovator of faith, working from the ground up, the inside out. He wore a habit of sackcloth stained with salt, he begged and spoke as if he were an ocean leading the foothills and mountains and rivers back toward their origins. To taste of the ocean's depth was to savour the word of God.

I can't help but equate Francis with Job, with Father's ashes, dust, and the unexpected life. Francis became the ashes that surrounded the diamonds of his time. He recognized in the ashes a place where to grieve is a necessary element in the restoration of faith and society. I imagine poetry, like prayer, like a time of ashes, as a recognition of the diamond at the centre of our lives. Wounds are entry points to this recognition. Each prayer, like a poem, lifts what is recognized into voice.

Studying the many souvenir concessions that line the streets of Assisi, storefronts that deal in religious trinkets and crafts depicting the life of Francis, I see it is easier to keep Francis in the bird bath, talking with the winged ones, the wolves, the flowers and trees, than to discuss his callused feet, the dirt beneath his fingernails, the stench of sacrifice, or his death in the hills. Francis's life and death were closer to the vigilant howl of a peacemaker, a smasher of demons and corruption, than to a poster boy for the wilderness. He lifted not just one prayer, his prayer, but the undirected prayers of a generation. There was nothing romantic about his decision to go broke and praise.

Father's decision to take up paint and canvas went against what was expected of him by his parents. Groomed in private schools and then university for a life of business or medicine, Father skipped out one day with Mother and spent at afternoon in the Rosedale Valley ravine painting close-ups of trees and bark and autumn leaves. Mother sat topless, holding an orange in her hand. When Father informed his parents of his decision to leave university, his own father threatened to cut him off, disown him, leave him to his own resources. Do what you have to do, Father replied. That was it. Mother and Father were on their own, Rachel Carson's *Silent Spring* in one hand, the complete works of Dylan Thomas in the other. They found in the cry and music of their own generation a sense of emerging justice, social change, and celebration. They took in the music of their age, Dylan and The Band at Le Coq d'Or, Mitchell and Cockburn at the Riverboat. Father's parents never did fully disown him, and never really did grasp the meaning of his paint and craft, how the world was blessed through his arms and hands. I remember the rare visits we made to my grandparents' Moore Park home, plastic coverings pulled tight over the furniture. There was nowhere to sit without feeling the world had come to an abrupt close.

In all my thoughts and feelings and actions, am I cultivating wisdom, reworking a place of devotion and character and capacity as Francis took on the rebuilding of the Chapel of San Damiano? Christ on the wooden cross above the broken altar speaks to his beloved: Francis, go and restore my house, which, as you see, is going to ruin.

What else? There were times following Mother's death when Father and I would stand outside churches, Father shaking his head. He couldn't go inside anymore and face that cross. Suddenly he was dry, he said. These churches we stood before, old dried-up wineskins. "Useless," he murmured. Father wanted juice after Mother's death, God, he wanted new blood, a complete transfusion.

For a time the narrative of Father's works, his paint and canvases, faded into deep blue, then dark, dark grey. His close-ups of oranges shrivelled, their skins so tight they seemed cut off from a source of light.

There are beggars of time, beggars of thirst, and beggars of howl. Father begged all three. Then he turned to the forests for his religion, where the thrust of life is self-organizing and ever-evolving. Here, he witnessed the greening of nature's sex seeking sun and sky again and again, whether the named be named or not. Once in the woods, Father made me promise that when his time came I'd cremate him, like Mother, like his fire-swept forests. I could do with his ashes as I pleased. I could smudge them over my skin or spread them over the wide world. I could give his remains to the many soils that suffered through the plight of industrial indifference where the earth had been seared, logged, and mined, and now required the potent force of ash, the black science of grief.

I take a measure of Father's ashes and mix them with an equal measure of soil from the garden outside the restored church of San Damiano. The mixture glows like a lantern on a tabletop.

Ana, I'm lying on the great lawn stretching down toward the Basilica of St. Francis. My eyes wander the deep, night skies, the world here draped in stars. There is a weightlessness within my chest, a sense that I am looking out at that which gave birth to us so many years ago.

A couple, Giovanni and Lucia, sit nearby on two fold-out chairs. Giovanni with bow and cello, Lucia with finger and violin. They tune their instruments, sitting in the quiet. They nod their heads, they align their bodies, minds and hearts with cello and violin, then peer up at the thick array of stars, the world above moving without a sound. Now and then a star falls, sweetly, toward the horizon. I follow the star's blaze until it becomes a thin thread of light fading across the sky, dying out. Giovanni pulls the bow across a string, releasing a soft, languid note. Another star falls, and another, and Lucia, here and there, plucks a string, a simple chord. Then silence. Then another falling star and a note of cello and violin, here and there, falling and playing, plucking and falling. I listen deeply. My eyes slide from stars to strings, strings to stars, falling and playing, flaring and fading, as this couple offer their night lessons and riff on the falling stars, jam away with the whole of the cosmos. There are notes of celebration; I am born. There are notes of requiem; I will die. And a note of love; thank God for the stars that teach us this.

FIRENZE

It's a good five-day walk from Assisi to Florence. Hills, roads, the Arno unfolding like a scroll. I arrive for one reason. To sit with Michelangelo's *David*. To look deeply into the rippling torso and belly, the great limbs like aqueducts conveying seed and sap. How even the foundational quiet of his stance and feet have the ability to seize my eyes and arrest my mind. No wonder so many men fear the inner life of marble. It changes how you stand.

After paying for a room and a handful of tin-box prayers, three days of rain and a bottle of wine, gazing into the corridors of *David*'s great eyes, there is nothing more of my sorrow and soul to hoard.

WHEAT FIELD WITH CROWS

The night train from Florence to Arles lets out at dawn. I leave the station on foot and walk west through Van Gogh's foothills, through a world of old footprints and faded irises and wheat fields full with crows. I place each of my steps like a flower petal upon the earth.

Father believed that the grief he felt following Mother's death could be pinned down by a single strand of her hair, such was the weight of his early sorrow. Yet Father imagined that if one were to weigh the gift of praise it would be like holding a Van Gogh canvas in one's hands, the weight of irises, their long stems spilling from earth. Father didn't want to confuse praise with only sunlight or weightlessness. He felt praise needed to be physically lifted, the whole of the body in on the act. The pull of each dark muscle, the curve and strain of creation.

But to become caught up in Van Gogh's works, to walk the land he praised and painted, is to understand why it was that the first wonder God created was light. The unseen brought into a powerful and colourful being. A light with the buoyancy of a lover's eye. The birthmarks of old stars mapping the way.

CAMINO DE SANTIAGO

For close to twelve hundred years people, husbands and wives and children, lovers and saints and fools, kings and queens, the rich, the poor, all pilgrim travellers, have left their homes and origins for these starlit roads that wind west toward Santiago de Compostela. This ancient city on the western tip of Spain, close to the end of the earth: Finisterre. I walk this road now strong as bone, the elements wrapped in a foot inside a boot. My shoulders tip with the weight of a packsack, my eyes aligned with the horizon. Spirit pulls the path from rock. I've heard that criminals in medieval Belgium, when convicted, were given a choice: do time in a local prison, or take to the road for Santiago. In the twelfth century this was no easy task. Days and nights without maps, the relentless heat and fears, the scarcity of modern conveniences. Other robbers and bandits and pilgrims along the way. This was Old Europe's version of the Wild West. Walking alone, with such uncertainty, could be a death sentence. Or it could be the unveiling of a whole new life, the heart revealed along an open road.

I've been on the road from Le Puy three weeks now. Today's roads are sparse and unkempt, overgrown with aging grasses and dry fennel. Autumn is approaching but the day-lit hours still swell with summer's heat. I follow the cut of the Lot River, in and out of its rushing presence. I haven't seen another soul for days. Against a wild oak tree I find a hip-high stick that fits into the palm of my hand, a perfect walking tool for the journey. I glance over the pilgrim guidebook I picked up in Rome and follow the stories of the thousands upon thousands who have walked this way. I dip down into fragrant valleys soaked in morning dew and back up along ragged cliffs and peaks, the sun in sway. The hours pass without seriousness. Here and there a broken chapel holds its door open to shade and rest. I walk sensing limits will be transcended, trusting in what I cannot see ahead. Each step rises out of the deep past and moves toward a deeper future. Hope charges out of the lap of what has been lost. Lost history, lost time, lost faith, the burned place. Go slow, be gentle, the road asks of the pilgrim.

Somewhere between Figeac and Cahors. I arrive in a village no larger than a thumbprint. One café/hotel, a church, a *tabac*, a small schoolhouse, and a few adjacent neighbourhoods. Plane trees line the main road and offer adequate cover. The cobblestone road runs away into the ploughed fields. This, and the quiet of the midday heat.

My body is hot. I feel worked in, like an old shoe. With so much walking, and the weight of the packsack against my shoulder blades and lower back, it's as if I'm slowly being ground into the earth. Twenty to twenty-five kilometres a day. I rise at six, pull cold water over my face and through my hair. Beard whiskers strong as tropical grass. Sometimes when I become overly tired, there's an acuity to my flesh, beyond time, beyond what I think I can endure.

I rest on the café patio, sitting back against a cool, green-blue wall. There's shade from the overhang of the roof and trellis. I savour a glass of water, a café au lait, bread and jam and cheese. My muscles still twitch with the road, a prehistoric joy. I wipe my hand through my hair, feel the perspiration, smell the odour of straw from my straw hat. I slept last night, out in the woods in a lean-to, next to a cemetery. There were graves two and three hundred years old. Inside an abandoned chapel in the cemetery there was an empty wooden altar crowned by a carving of a descending dove. The baptismal font was filled with dust and cobwebs, threads of worship, sanctuary, and decay. I found a candle stub, greying wax displaced over the altar, a hard black wick. I lit the candle and felt the heat of the flame against my dampened fingertips. Then I pressed the flame out while smudging some of Father's ashes—loose, warm loam—into the melted wax. I worked the wax and ashes back into the candle stub, fresh with Father's seal. I lit the candle again and watched its light pulse through the open window.

I'll stay here the night, I think, get a room in the hotel, spend the afternoon siesta in a bed. A hot bath would be nice.

The woman who serves me on the patio is the same woman who manages the hotel. She's a solid-looking woman, bold, hair blue-grey, a face bent on hard work. She waits for me to speak.

"Do you have a room?" I ask, my French halting.

A row of keys dangle from a rack at her back. She twists her face, an undersized peach, and looks me up and down. My hard whiskers, my soiled hair, my dirty T-shirt and dust-covered hiking boots.

"*Un moment*," she says.

She turns into a backroom, behind a curtain. I can hear her whispering with a man, two voices, like twins, whispering near a sideboard where there must be some china because the porcelain amplifies their whispers.

The woman reappears from behind the curtain, looks at me, and waves a finger.

"*Complet*," she announces, one hand on hip.

"But all those keys . . ."

"*Complet*," she says again, waving the finger.

Then she explains that a bus can take me ahead to Cahors or back to Figeac. In those towns there are many hotels, plenty of room.

"I'm on foot, I'm walking," I say. "I'm a pilgrim (*Je suis pèlerin*!). I'm on my way to Santiago de Compostela. Cars and buses and trains are now out of the question."

The woman shakes her head and waves that finger, all five digits. She tells me there haven't been any pilgrims through here in years, decades. I look like a wanderer to her, too dirty to be a pilgrim. A hippy.

I sit again on the patio. More water, a ham and cheese omelette, a second café au lait. One o'clock and twenty-eight degrees. The sun breaks up the shade, a dog is on the prowl. No one in the village is moving. The salt of my sweat bares a strange thirst.

I make my way to the local church. The insides are cool and empty, a reprieve from the heat. I look around, knock on the sacristy door but there's no one inside. My footsteps sound off on the stone floor. I sit in a pew and hum an old tune: I'm fixing a hole where the rain gets in and stops my mind from wandering where it will go-oh. My voice trails over discoloured walls, through statues of saints without fingers.

I rest an hour in the pew, then wake to the sound of my own breathing. A jolt. A car pulls up outside the church, wheels turning over gravel. A man gets out of the car and enters the church, stops at the holy water, wets a finger, and makes the sign of the cross. He spots my packsack and walking stick by the door, then scans the pews and finds me there, half in darkness. He looks to the packsack again, then back to me, and approaches me, slowly.

He doesn't hesitate to ask, "You are having problems?"

"I'm waiting for the priest," I say. "I thought you might be the priest."

"Oh no no," he says, "there is no priest living in this village. I'm the organist. Raymond, Raymond de la Fontaine. You are looking for a place to stay, is that it?"

"Yes," I say. "The hotel is apparently full."

"I saw the packsack. It is your packsack?"

"Yes."

"Where are you headed?" he asks.

"I hope to reach Santiago," I say. "If I last that long."

Raymond pauses and steps back, placing his fingers over his lips.

"Most who pass through now are only hikers," he then says, "out for a Sunday walk. But you, you're a pilgrim?"

"I'm trying," I say.

"Years, years," he says, "since I've seen anyone walking through here on their way to Santiago."

His eyes moisten.

"If you don't mind," he says, "I will practise on the organ and then I will take care of you. Will this help you?"

"More than you know," I say.

He begins to step away toward the organ.

"Dara," I say.

"Oui."

"My name. It's Dara."

"Enchanté," Raymond says.

Raymond takes to the organ, music his balm. He plays evenly, excitedly, often peering back over his shoulder to see if I am still there.

It is a whirlwind night. Raymond invites me to stay at his home, have dinner with him and his wife, Catherine. A home-cooked meal, a feast in a dining room where the white walls are marked with black-and-white photographs of bridges, bridges rebuilt after the war, spanning Western Europe.

"I was a young man," Raymond says. "A young engineer. We could not escape what happened in the war, but bridge-building helped ease the gap between victory and defeat, between suffering and redemption. You understand?"

We eat fresh pâté, salami on bread, a green salad, too much wine; then a small serving of roast chicken and roasted carrots and potatoes, more wine; followed by fresh figs and blackberries in a thick cream sauce; coffee and a bowl of apricots to follow in the garden. We sit among the poplars. Raymond spreads out his maps to Santiago, shows me the many routes through France, up through the Pyrenees, the heights. He suggests I keep making my way along this route to Saint-Jean-Pied-de-Port; insists finally.

"The stars swarm the mountains at night," he says. "Bare rock with a heavenly shine."

They've been to Santiago once, by car, a few years ago. It's not the same as doing it by foot, Raymond smiles. But in two years' time he and Catherine plan to walk, step out their front door, shake loose forty years of domestic life, and go. They do not regret a moment of their family and working life, four children, forty bridges, and a garden.

Catherine, sitting in a lawn chair, lifts her feet and shakes them in the air, as if walking up a hillside. She's been preparing her legs and feet for a year now, walking five kilometres a day with a packsack weighted down with stones from the garden.

"I'm so used to the stones," she says, "I think I'll take them to Santiago as well."

The night sky hums with the life force of a coming moon, giving off the same light as that by the apricot in the palm of my hand.

Catherine asks if I'd prefer a cold chicken sandwich for my lunch on the road the next day, or just a fresh tomato, a baguette, and cheese to carry.

"Or a little of everything," Raymond says.

I'm given a guest room with a window that looks onto the backyard and a long row of poplars, rustling now in the night winds. Beyond the treeline I can see the steep ridges surrounding the Lot, a crescent moon there like the mark of a lover's kiss upon a beloved's neckline. I organize my pack-sack, shifting items, working toward a compact balance. I ease into bed, feeling the light touch of possibility. Ana in a prayer.

A gentle breeze slips through the window, drops morning light at the foot of the bed. Fluorescent sheaves work their way under the sheet, along my waking skin.

We share a simple breakfast of fruit, cheese, a baguette, jam, and coffee. Raymond and Catherine drive me back to the church. Raymond asks of us to go inside and make a prayer, insisting on an old local tradition of blessing those pilgrims making their way on foot to Santiago. The pilgrim carries the hopes and prayers and sorrows of those who must stay behind.

"In Santiago," Raymond tells me, "you will find in the cathedral a statue of the Apostle saint, Santiago himself. It's an awkward-looking thing, very ornate, placed some paces behind the altar and up a few stairs. One must climb to find the saint. Once there, custom has it that the pilgrim must hug the saint from behind, wrapping your arms around his great bejewelled shoulders, while gazing into the cathedral, back over the altar and into the faces of the other pilgrims and travellers of the way."

Raymond pauses, and looks me in the eye.

"We didn't hug the Apostle when we were there," he confides, "because we didn't walk the way. We drove. But I sensed as I witnessed those pilgrims hug that saint, looking into their eyes as they looked back over the altar into our eyes, that something in their lives had shifted."

"All we ask," Catherine leans in and whispers to me, "is that when you hug the Apostle you remember us, as we will remember you when we too make the journey."

I promise. I will be their bridge, the way Father's ashes have been mine.

Catherine gives me a paper bag containing sandwiches and fruit for the road. Raymond then presents me with a scallop shell, the ancient badge of the pilgrim, when in days of old the pilgrim would reach Santiago then venture a few more days to the Atlantic, Finisterre, at land's end, and there gather a shell from the ocean as proof of their journey. Raymond also gives me a bottle of wine from his cellar. The bottle is unmarked and the wine inside is dark as the cellar wherein it has been stored. The cork smells like a handful of grapes thrown open to the sun.

"I know it's a little more weight to carry," Raymond says of the wine. "But we can't help wanting to provide for you. This is a time when your appetite must be met. Your health."

The way I receive their hospitality and the warm hugs Raymond and Catherine give comes spilling through my body with all the liberating force of a Sunday morning.

"*Merci*," I offer, my eyes tearing. "*Merci beaucoup*."

The hillsides and fields are so full of sunlight today, it's almost unsettling. A slow morning walk of ridge and valley, valley and ridge. The heat pressing me into place. Close to noon I descend into Cahors along a steep track of white rock and scrub brush. The city makes its three-sided nest along a great curve of the Lot River. I make my way to the cathedral in the city's centre. It's market day. Covered stalls fill the square and parking spaces by the cathedral. I stock up on fruit and cheese and nuts. I sit inside the cathedral and sink into the blessed silence. I make my way through the city core, west along Rue Wilson, and cross the Pont Valentré, an ancient Roman bridge. The bridge is fortified and the Lot drives beneath is wide arches, crisp and quick and deliberate. It's the river that speaks to the pilgrim about endurance. I climb the steep rock cliff out of the city and slope my way along a tight ridge to the Croix de Magne, a look out back over Cahors and the Lot. I eat quietly. These are the days in their unfolding. A supple heart. The mind relaxed.

There's something about the early morning hours in the valleys of the Lot. The soft, milky mists. The patient sky. The coo of the mourning dove. All make for an effortless pace.

I happen upon a small chapel (Saint-Jean-le-Froid) nestled in a grove of poplars next to a field of aging sunflowers. The sunflower stems are thick and angled like the broad backs of monks tending mid-morning office. Inside the chapel there is a small stone altar and a single pine bench before it. The chapel is well swept, the altar prepared with wildflowers—purple, yellow, orange. There is an open book, a guest ledger upon a side table. Fingerprints the colour of copper across each page. Hundreds of names are entered in the ledger, supported by blue lines. A testimony to a date and time of a pilgrim's walking this same narrow path along this crease in the world leading to Santiago. Each name rises and touches my eyes. I'm no longer a stranger to this undulant landscape, these blue lines. I've been here before, under another name.

As I walk I sense the bloodline of the ancients. Old World bones. Neolithic sediment. I see polished veins two metres beneath the earth, underworld currents. Rivulets. Here, from Cahors to Montcuq to the medieval village of Lauzerte, toward Moissac, I encounter the ink of blood and memory that honours the core of the Western canon, working spirit into mind, into matter, and back. My hands are at the mercy of history, literature, this land made holy in heat and rain. I've thinned out like a burnt root. I've aged like a clay bowl glazed with sun. I've searched rock and wood for the ring of completion, of recognition, the flint of consciousness. At every step and bend there is the terror of my own fragility. My body is too small to eclipse time, decay, and the moon.

I rest a day in Moissac. I bathe in the balm of the Abbey of Saint-Pierre. I walk its cloister, get lost in the lives of the saints and the biblical stories etched into its many edged stone columns and capitals. Even in the telling quiet of a stone story, language is a profound responsibility.

Leaving Moissac after dawn, I walk along a tree-lined gravel path next to the river Tarn and meet a young man named Josef. He's navigating his way toward me with a donkey weighed down with packsacks and camping gear. He's making his way back to his home in Munich, having left there a year or so earlier for Santiago. He began the journey with his wife, Maria, and the donkey. A few weeks into the walk they found Maria to be pregnant. They continued their pilgrimage, Maria's belly growing full with child. A week after their arrival in the holy city she gave birth to a son. Josef smiles a big, wide black-bearded smile. "No need to ask," he then says, "we couldn't help but name the child Jesus."

Mother Maria and the baby Jesus flew on ahead home.

I invite Josef to sit with me by the river. We lay out a small spread of fruit and cheese and bread. I open the bottle of wine Raymond gave me. I sniff the cork, as does Josef, then let the wine breathe. The waters of the Tarn shine past, dappled lines of morning light coming through the trees. I pour two glasses of wine. Josef and I eye to eye, toasting the new day.

Prost!

I'm following the story of a saint, a field, and a star. Something mythical gropes in my throat. How one night long ago a shepherd tending his flock in Western Spain had his life changed in a singular bright moment of ecstatic release. He witnessed a star moving low over the earth, as if picking out a point in a field that had been ordained, that must be dug. So he followed that star and found that point of earth and he dug and he dug, and to his delight he found the buried remains of Santiago—the Apostle James. Bones there intimately connected to the story of the Christ, bones that became the first pillars to a cathedral and a road. This wild way laid before me all because of a shepherd's sacred high.

As I walk these roads into the foothills of the Pyrenees, I sense the years in cultivation, the births and deaths, battles and song, that mark the way. A mapped world slowly coming into view. Then the mountains themselves suddenly get in behind my eyes before I can complete my next step and breath. I have to stop and gather my senses, my heart stunned. Each peak is a wing held in upward motion, sustaining the flow of the entire mountain range. Powerful black-tipped silhouettes. Clouds appearing and disappearing, their soft shadows extending for miles.

Saint-Jean-Pied-de-Port is cradled in the Pyrenees, taking in the steep, soaking rays of sun. I've entered a landscape of pure unfolding. I cannot say if I've reached a fresh meaning or am only passing through here. This morning the walk from Saint-Palais to Saint-Jean consisted of mist and rain, low-lying cloud cover. Angled tree trunks pointed the way. Close to noon the system had lifted, the Pyrenees stripped of their garments. I thought, *If I die here in these foothills it will be enough*.

I find a place of refuge on the edge of the old town, a small room in a house that serves as a place of hospitality for pilgrims. Just me in a room with six beds. It's late in the season for pilgrims on foot, I'm told by a woman who admits me and has me sign a register in which all the names of those who have walked to Santiago are entered. Then she gives me a pocket passport which I am to use along the way, the passport being a kind of ticket to other places of hospitality, and proof of my journey. The woman stamps the passport with the seal of Saint-Jean-Pied-de-Port, gives me a blessing, and leaves me alone. The mountains seem to descend, freely burning bright, through the only window in the room. I sleep an hour, a towel against the heat over my eyes. Daydreams prepare me for tomorrow's climb. A baptism of fire, the woman has warned me. Take lots of water.

I eat an early dinner in a pizzeria just off the main thoroughfare. I sit with a view of mountain passes and the gate of Notre Dame through which I must pass to begin my morning climb. From there it will be all mountain air and the salt of my sweat working through my skin and shirt. I eat slowly, honouring each bite. I'm aware of the energy I must take in, store, and process for the morning climb.

The last of the season's tourists amble about, aimless, without concern. Market stalls are still open along the main street, merchants and artisans sell crafts and trinkets, the local cheese and wine. Ana, I'm watching the back of a young woman. She's selling jewellery from behind a stall. She sits on a small crate, head and shoulders just above the table top. She is small, the back of her arms and legs are well tanned. Her hair is the colour of summer wheat. A young man with a ponytail approaches her. He leans over her shoulder and smiles in profile. He hugs her gently and lays his head on her shoulder while his right arm and hand caress her from the side, his hand slipping beneath her T-shirt, touching her rib cage, up toward her breast. The young woman remains still, revealed and not abandoned. After a moment she stands and steps away to help a customer. She doesn't adjust her T-shirt. The young man sits back on the wooden crate and lights a cigarette.

Ana, what is it about this couple's loving gestures that wash over my senses? My hands have crossed your belly and breasts to find these hillside towns. At the core of my loving you my heart is no longer solo on its path, your tender lyric infusing my blood.

Does peace arise in opposition to sorrow and suffering? Or is it a gift always and already enwrapped within the grieving heart? Is suffering then a midwife for peace? As music birthed through silence, attunement, and your breath.

I wake refreshed, the cool night airs having calmed my sleep. I leave Saint-Jean-Pied-de-Port without looking back. I step down the old cobblestone road and through the gates of Notre Dame, cross the river Nive and step up rue d'Espagne. A prayer with each firm step. I pass through the gate that the Romans and Charlemagne and Napoleon passed through; I move with the ghosts of armies and pilgrims, up into the heights, through glacial marks and wandering mists. The tops of the mountains are concealed by clouds. I see the counterpoint of an approaching light in the dense green undergrowth. I hear tiny bells jangling on sheep as they step among barren rock. Grasses are chewed down to their wine-coloured roots. My body stings with the pull of an old-growth forest, pulling as I climb. Clouds and mists slowly dissolve, only to reveal still more heights. In the mountain clefts I see the eagle's perch. Morning stars turn toward the sun. Rock face plunges below, disappears. All threats of vertigo leave my mind. The climb pierces my heart the way these peaks pierce the open sky. With each upward step and surge I sense a world once formless and void, dark and divine, clinging to my body like sea salt, like moonlight on leaves. I crest the peak and walk on in silence, the ascent like a sweet, sweet elixir.

Mountain work is good and hard and necessary, Father Daniel shared with me. It is also essential to return to the valley and do the good and hard work of love and healing.

I step down through the tipping forest and into the monastic hamlet of Roncesvalles and find a stirring of the ages. After thirty-three kilometres and ten hours of climbing and descending, I arrive in this awkward place as if after a journey of eight hundred years. Time tilts its tired head back in the shade of the great church carved out of the side of the hamlet's mountains. A church open to the pilgrim, centuries of hospitality and the wind. Once, to enter Spain was to enter the last vestiges of the known world. One then travelled westward over seven hundred kilometres through pastures and vineyards and further mountain ranges before reaching what was once believed to be the end of the earth, the coast where the Atlantic swayed, its white mist of salt and spray distinguishing the Old World from the New.

Roncesvalles was once the most powerful monastery in the region, its influence reaching through the lands of Navarra and beyond. It was refuge for the pilgrim, taking thousands in throughout the Middle Ages. Now the monastery sleeps through its days and nights, unspoiled by the visitor, adjacent to a hamlet with two streets, a tavern, and a small hotel.

I arrive to the sound of dogs barking. Two elderly monks sit, their heads heavy on their shoulders, on a stone bench beneath an archway. The sky surrounding the church is light blue and warm to the eye. Brown leaves lie scattered on the cobblestone road, each leaf containing a manner of death as my body contains its own. One more step and I would have sunk from exhaustion.

I am greeted by a small, enthusiastic priest. He speaks with emotion and conviction, his name flying over my head. He seems a full foot taller, more voluminous, than his slight frame suggests. Eager to take me in, to stamp my pilgrim passport with the seal of the Virgin of Roncesvalles, he escorts me into a small office in the back of the monastery and doesn't stop talking for the better part of an hour. His tongue moves swiftly between Spanish, French, and English. My ears wade through his words, the things I am expected to understand about the walk ahead: the sacredness of the way, what I might witness; a change in weather, a change of heart, a change in how I walk.

"Walking restores meaning to God's balance," he says.

Then he asks me to hold out my hand and make a fist. This I do.

"Often in life we get like this," he says, also making a fist. "We contract and tighten up and stay like this, and come to believe it is normal to live like this. Now slowly open your hand."

This we do together, unfolding our fists from the fingertips, opening out our palms, then resting with an open hand, facing upwards.

"You see, this is the natural position of the hand. This takes no effort. But the fist, that takes effort. This," he says, showing me his open hand and palm once again. "This is the Camino. This is the path of the open heart."

I stay the night in the monastery, in a third-floor room with twenty bunk beds and no other person. I sleep on a soft, springy mattress. The windows are thrown open onto the cooling mountains. I have a cold shower, followed by a meal of eggs and toast and wine in a tavern. Later, I attend a benediction Mass for the pilgrim in the church. Every night for hundreds of years, without interruption, this Mass has been celebrated. The church is spacious, candlelit, full of sacred cups and candelabrum. The altar is a tangle of silver and precious stone, the Virgin of Roncesvalles there with her gleaming eye. Eight monks, flourishing in white, hands held high, celebrate Mass. The aroma and mist of incense works through their trance of prayer and thanksgiving.

"Rejoice with Jerusalem, Isaiah says," the monks intone. "Be glad for her, all you who love her! Rejoice, rejoice with her, all you who mourn her! So that you may be suckled and satisfied from her consoling breast, so that you may drink deep with delight from her generous nipple."

I sleep well, nourished by a dream of rain.

Bells announce the morning's journey. Each of my steps now resemble the sacred moods I move through between my tongue and God's ear.

Leaving has become my returning. To be at home on the road is to be filled. Every breath is imbued with meaning. I have walked knowing I have willingly abandoned what I once knew as home. I have walked, like Father, a beggar of howl. I have walked, holding these ashes rolled up now in the leather medicine pouch, soft as a sprig, as if gripping a divining rod used to discern where it is heaven and earth are enfolded in love. I have walked the world of roads, of human and non-human traffic, where lands have cleansed my mind and the insides of my skullcap, which had been ravaged by weather patterns and black ice. I have walked knowing home is no longer a place marked by permanence; it is contained in the point of departure which itself contains the point of return, the way fruit contains its seed.

It's been six hours and twenty-five kilometres of road, Roncesvalles to Zubiri. Noon hour and hot. Zubiri is thick with exhaust, a quick highway cutting through its centre, dividing its core. Its hills gape with the ravages of industry, smog twisting overhead like displaced halos. I find a cool spot by a shallow river, between the shadows cast by an old Roman bridge. I drink a litre of water, take in an apple, a slice of cheese and bread. Something about the shade here feels under pressure, a hand around a throat. Smokestacks in the distance pull at complex elements stashed within the hills. Loudspeakers have replaced the bells in the church tower. The dismantling of grace, a crushed riverbed.

All roads that slip like rain from leaf and branch, dripping toward Santiago, become one in Puente la Reina. The red of these roads seeps into the red of my blood.

It's a good afternoon to walk. The heat is down. The air is striking and clear. I move along an easy stretch of road through Pamplona, toward Cizur Menor, then make the steady climb through green and brown hills toward the Alto del Perdón. Villages below (Uterga, Obanos, Puente la Reina) rest under a mantle of constellations, tucked into the coming dusk. Pamplona was busy, its citizens in a post-siesta jig, in and around streets and fountains, huddling at café tables, talking, sharing in sweets and coffee, beer, wine, the usual sustenance of ordinary saints. A man stopped me as I passed along Calle Mayor, treated me to a small cup of beer and tapas, then patted me on the back, smiling. "Give my regards to the Apostle," he said. This land has been washed through by years of hard sun, worked and reworked by tumbling rock and water. The road is a cradle of gravel, stone, large boulders, and wheat trampled underfoot. Stark, vivid browns spill forward over the tilled earth. There is a greening in the distance so subtle I take it for something undergoing consecration. Soils mingle with dark roots, particles gleam like the small table lamps used by monks to study ancient manuscripts of hearts, minds, and souls. Trees with faint branches rap against the skin of sky. The earth here is poised and still as a tabletop supporting a community of vines and wines. Rioja's wines. There's a stillness when walking, the long hours on foot shedding the last step. It is one thing to walk knowing sorrow has been transmuted, the way the prophets and masters teach. All that dead wood burned away. It is another thing to walk trusting in a son of man who has nowhere to lay his head. These ridges and mountains I've moved over, this autumn air in the falling night. Falling like the years I've misspent, mistaking sin for spring, stone for water. There's nothing more beneath my dark heart but a faithful witness to the world as it is.

On the edge of Puente la Reina there stands a statue of a metal medieval pilgrim. He looks like he's stepped out of a cartoon; a wide triangular hat, a dark cape, the scallop shell that pilgrims wore to distinguish who they were and a shepherd's crook with a gourd for water or wine. He's angled in a peculiar position of welcome.

Midnight in the refuge. The village outside the window is unclouded and calm. There are three other pilgrims here, well asleep. I organize myself in the darkness and fall back on the mattress, sink in. I am reassured by another's soft breath, the easy pace of a pilgrim's snoring.

Sleep works its way through my body from head to toe, like bracelets of pollen drifting downstream.

The morning appears over Puente la Reina as a blue-grey mist, the road displaced by a hard rain. The day is washed out, filling cups with solitude. The priest from the local church ducks through the doorway. He holds a jacket overhead, while balancing in a free hand a tray with coffee and bread and a stamp for our pilgrim passports. He shares with us a tale of the many winds and rains which have been unable to alter the foundations of the town's Romanesque bridge for over twelve hundred years. The bridge is outside the window, its stone the colour of whitened wheat. Cracks have been replaced with cement, silver and gold. Even in the rain, the bridge glitters. The river Arga crashes beneath its six heavy arches. These are the first rains in weeks. The sun comes through by mid-afternoon and the priest invites us to stay another night. I'm tempted to carry on, cross that bridge into the newly soaked roads and landscapes beyond.

But I stay on.

Carlos and Suzanna Lopez married last weekend in Madrid. They took a train from Madrid to Pamplona and began walking. A honeymoon on the road, on foot, a four-or-five-day excursion from Pamplona to Logrono. Carlos is a chiropractor; Suzanna a massage therapist. After a day's journey, its many uneven steps, the night is a time of cracking, adjusting the spine, realigning the skeleton. Their working hands are bold, yet intimate as a flowerpot.

Daniel James Langan is of Irish descent. "Just call me Jim," he says. He's been on the road for two months, beginning his walk in Chartres. Bearded, hair tempered by sun, pulled back into a ponytail. He wears a T-shirt with the image of a beaming Mickey Mouse covering his chest from neck to waist. "Found it in a monastery in France, in the lost and found," he says, "couldn't resist his smile." The T-shirt is extra large, hangs like a skirt over Jim's waist, sways as he walks. His packsack is weighted with clothing, sleeping bag, camera equipment, a large black notebook for sketching and words, a flute, and a guitar strapped along its side.

We spend a few days walking with one another, four for the road. Puente la Reina to Estella to Los Arcos, Los Arcos to Logrono. Each day has its rare rhythm, arising with dawn in the furrowed fields. We pass churned soils enfolding vines pruned by the wind, by the hands of migrant workers whose faces appear each morning like moons from behind dark grape leaves. It's impossible to escape the honesty of each step. Our conversations swing and drift and flow along the influential currents that connect us to this land, the constellations mapped by the blazing Spanish mind; Picasso, Goya, Lorca; St. John of the Cross and Teresa of Avila. We share in fruit and nuts and liquids along the hearth that is this road. It is a walk harnessed by confessions of personal collisions, wailing walls where human hurts and prayers are tucked. The flesh of faith. This is where we encounter ourselves, then forget ourselves, welcoming the root-fires of regeneration as we step along the way.

We lose our direction between Estella and Los Arcos, road and map disagreeing. Waymarkers along the path are obscured or missing, trampled under. What was supposed to be a short morning turns long, four hours off course. We retrace our steps and try other ways and turns. We move through lowlands cradled between great dinosaur-like ridges where monastic ruins cling to fault lines. The valleys are full of a gold, bright wheat, awaiting the harvest. To ease our being lost, Jim strums his guitar, humming everything from the Beatles to U2, Cohen to Dylan. Carlos and Suzanna lick their index fingers and hold them in the air, testing direction.

Near the outskirts of Los Arcos there are advertisements nailed to dead trees, the sides of abandoned homes, and hydro poles. Each advertisement promises the best for the pilgrim at the best prices in town at the best bar/hotel/restaurant in the region. It's where the locals go. But when we enter Los Arcos, the town seems lean and blotted out by sun. Trucks pass through the main thoroughfare and do not stop. In the only bar in the only hotel and restaurant, the TV groans. Its sound echoes off hard-tiled walls and floors. Exhausted sounds of the world news, that warning to Saddam Hussein, *Get out of Kuwait or else!* We wait twenty minutes, bodies tired. Locals arrive, take their seats round the TV, are served their beers and tapas within minutes. The waiter refuses to make eye contact with us. Carlos gets up, rolls his neck, then moves across the room through a ring of cigarette smoke. He starts up a slow, deliberate conversation with the waiter. Carlos returns with a promise of food and drink. We wait. Ten, twenty minutes. The yellow fields beyond take on pink. Suzanna stirs, lifts her hand, and waves for the waiter. He looks at her, then turns back to the television.

The pilgrim is a stranger, moves in a landscape half accomplished, half unaccomplished. What the pilgrim's heart offers is a space to lay our prayers and longings, an altar upon which to set a jug of wine and a few glasses. If unwelcome, the pilgrim moves on, without worry, taking up the heart of a journey where the village roads have left off. The pilgrim moves in a world overcome with indecision, disbelief, a land after death. The religions of the world germinate at table tops and are wrapped like a secret scroll inside the pilgrim's step.

We find an abandoned shelter in the fields outside of town, a shepherd's lean-to. We share a meal of canned white asparagus, black olives, salami, cheese, bread, wine, oranges. The Milky Way slips overhead, pure, swimming the zenith. We sleep the night on makeshift beds of hay. I open my eyes at three. I imagine Ana's scent of prayer like a psalm in its fiery orbit, finding me. There was a time when I would have thought I didn't depend on any of this, that it was enough to know the names of constellations and the order of objects in a room. That I could keep rivers and trees and seas and the sun at a congenial distance. That a sense of self stopped at my skin. It used to be I did not experience the elements as a grace through which seas were lifted and clouds were formed and rains returned to our bodies, inspiring a taste for the numinous life. I rest now in a world cradled by great waters and the pull of an undertow beneath my breast, cultivating immense presence.

Jim and I see Carlos and Suzanna off at the bus station in Logrono. Jim strums a song of farewell: may the wind always be at your back. Each of these partings becomes soil for the soul. The tongue is stilled in the blue silence of departure. Now, a simple embrace gives our stories away.

Logrono is festive. Church squares and cafés and bars are crowded and active. The night is cooling and loose. Sunday. A band plays in the Plaza del Mercado, piping tunes, songs buzzing the ear. Children appear from side streets, sweets in hand, skipping ropes, wearing extra-large sweaters. A small boy walks around with a box over his head. The cafés are full of parents and grandparents. Voices rise and tumble and spill.

Logrono owes its present to its past, the road to Santiago bringing with it pilgrims who became settlers. The town fans out from the river Ebro. Churches two or three blocks apart mark the way; Santa Maria del Palacio, Santiago el Real. Roads meander, imitating the river, laced with star-light. More often than not I find myself firm in my body, no longer retreating, but rising a little bit, the phoenix, up through Father's ashes. There is resolve in these roads; blood rivers the human heart.

The landscape from Logrono to Nájera, and beyond toward Burgos, is hard on the knees. It's a land that jolts, rock-filled and red. Jim and I walk, step for step. We share in an equal pace and quiet, marked by each sunrise and sunset, by fatigue and the blisters we tend on one another's feet. We move up sleeping Roman roads and slanted valley rises where vineyards spiral back into uneven horizons. Boulders lean against tree trunks like stone reliefs of shepherds. Jim can't help but use his camera, intoxicated with every angle of stone, leaf, and vine, until we have to walk along a two-lane highway and his eye comes across a crooked shape lying in a ditch next to a stone wall by a cemetery. A police officer is approaching the shape, a sheet in hand. He bends down, unfolds the sheet and covers the shape, then stands and walks away. People huddle quietly next to the road, heads down, still. A man leans against a slanted car, its wheels in the ditch. His head is turned away. Skid marks. Further along the ditch by the cemetery, a mountain bike is pressed up against the stone wall, handlebars bent, wheels forced at right angles, spokes protruding like splintered bone through skin, jammed back into the earth. Brake lines, gear lines, dangle like sinew. The crooked shape beneath the sheet belongs to a young woman. She had been heading to Santiago, struck while rounding a curve. "God bless her on her new road," Jim says. I rub a pinch of Father's ashes into the stone wall by the cemetery, between the young woman and her bike. Jim and I walk on, our tears reduced to whispers falling onto a red earth whose shadows we cannot interpret. If we dare turn to the language of shadows at all.

Santo Domingo de la Calzada appears in the distance of a yellowing valley and a river harnessed by sun. With each step closer, the city seems to pull back.

Mass in the Cathedral of Santo Domingo de la Calzada is accompanied by a strange beat, an unorthodox musical cutting through the old drone. As the priest intones the opening prayers and the congregation of aging men and women raise their voices in response, heads tilted every way but up, the whole cathedral is suddenly filled with the piercing, unwavering, high-pitched crowing of a cock. Jim and I turn our heads. In a gilded cage, Gothic, circus-like, set inside a wall, is the sacred hen and the sacred cock, crowing and strutting, praising as the priest moves through the Mass, lifting his cup and his bread. It's a love story gone wrong inside that cage, in that wild song. Four or five hundred years ago, three pilgrims from Germany—a mother, father, and son—stopped for food at a pilgrim's inn. The young woman serving them fell in love with the son. But the son did not return her love, and out of spite, or hurt, the young woman reported the son to the town magistrate, the charge being theft from the inn. The young son was taken prisoner and sentenced to death. The parents later made a plea with the magistrate. The magistrate sat at dinner, feasting on roast chicken. "Spare our son," the parents begged, "he's innocent." But the magistrate, enjoying his chicken, wiped his lips, and said, "Your son is hanged already, and besides,

your son is as innocent as this chicken on my plate is alive."
It is said that at that moment the thick, skinned chicken
regained its plumage and stepped off the plate, alive and
strutting, crowing. The mother and father and townspeople
bolted for the gallows where the hanging son was alive.

My heart is a cathedral strutting and crowing, wild in
love and lamentation.

Last night in a dream Father approached. His arms were
like the wings of a hawk, his eyes like imperfect pearls. He
handed me a map. He was with a woman. She might have
been Mother, or Elle. I wanted to recognize them, to say
their names. But they slipped through the dream like deer
through a hardwood forest. When I looked at the map, their
footprints where there, sealed, brilliant as seed germinating
in the palm of my hand.

Jim and I make the trek from Villafranca to San Juan
de Ortega, edging up the steep incline leaving Villafranca.
Hillsides are digested through to their primeval layers. Small
pine trees are flanked by grey rock, their branches loaded
with thick needles gesturing skyward. Then an oak forest
reveals its low, stubborn canopy and a sense of autumn's
emerging verse. This land with its baked geography and
years of scarring beneath a persistent heat. The climb
begins to take its toll on Jim's knees, tendons swelling, red.
Each step is now a raven circling the dead. Jim's left knee
seizes, impossible to bend. We move slowly and make it to

the fountain at Valdefuentes. An oasis. There is cool water brimming up from the earth's core and a handful of shade next to a hollow with a hermitage. Jim sits by the fountain and bathes his left knee, cup after cup of cold water over the swollen flesh. Carlos and Suzanna had shown us how to massage the tendons around the knees, so I try my hand at the technique, thumb and forefingers easing into the tendon just below the sore spot, stretching the tendon out. We wait a few hours, water up, share orange slices, bread, cheese, and enjoy a siesta. The sun eases behind the trees. We gather ourselves. Jim is sure he can make the rest of the walk to San Juan de Ortega, two or three hours. The road is straight, night-bright, a page fleshed out. We follow rock and early stars. Smoke rises from far-off houses as if from between two lines in a book of prose. Dusk whispers of a deeper creed. Our bodies tremble with the language learned in the bosom of a forest, a temple setting where tree limbs extend like the arms of mothers and fathers when their prodigal children return.

It's near eight when we arrive at San Juan de Ortega. There's nothing much to the town but an old church, a dorm for pilgrims, a few neighbouring houses, a café, and a soft drink machine leaning against a stone wall. We're welcomed by a priest right out of a Graham Greene novel, cigarette going, lips singed with the spoils of someone else's wine. He's been here so many years he's given up the need for measurement by numbers or the exchanging of names. He shakes our hands, asks us our places of origin, grins, comments on the night skies, looks to the soft drink machine, grins again, then hands us off to a small woman in black, hair grey and tight as a cringe. We must be hungry and thirsty and tired, she says. We're given our beds in an unheated dorm but the showers are warm. Then we're asked into the priest's kitchen where we're thrown open to the seduction of his wine. He pours us two glasses and asks us what we do back home. I say I'm in between jobs, and for now my focus is on Father's ashes, their holy distribution. He nods, knowingly. Jim admits that he's in between jobs as well and going forward he desires work that only enhances the beauty of life, and that is no longer determined to rip the planet apart from its ecological integrity. He's tired, he says, of humanity set on ravaging the earth of its dignity. The nihilistic notion that it's survival of the fittest or bust.

"I'm afraid to say you'll be waiting a long time for that to change," the priest says, pouring us more mine. "Now, let us eat."

He's prepared a traditional garlic soup, a taste taking the tongue back seven generations. There's no telling when an appetite for truth will find itself stirring in the pleasure of a meal, our bodies relaxing as if into a moment of pure reflection.

"Wherever two or more are gathered, I am there with them. Isn't that what Rabbi Jesus says?" the priest says, looking us in the eyes, patting the tabletop.

How long have I mistaken sorrow for the disorder of an imperfect hunger?

Mother and her unaccomplished mercy, the prayers she uttered on hands and knees, looking to lift her pain. The same prayers that now work through my loins. Father, his hands that eventually learned to be patient with grief and the music of a brush stroke. Each of his paintings then seemed to sing with the mystery of a lover's offering. And Elle, how she found the richness of communion in the midst of star showers. How the subtle arch of her spine along a hardwood floor taught her praise as we made love in the barn rafters of her youth.

I see my own journey through grief now, the slow undressing of its many colours. The blues, the blacks, the reds, the yellows, the greens. The soft surrender of my body as it undergoes its many descents and darknesses only to resurface thickened by love. I see the broken heart's cry for heaven's sky. Night rains on my breast.

Jim and I walk from San Juan de Ortega to Burgos knowing it is our last day together. Jim has enrolled in a course in Spanish, a four-month affair, into the new year. He'll complete the journey to Santiago in the early spring, wait the winter out.

So we walk in the manner of planets, trusting in the spaces between us. We're assured now in our orbit and the gravitational bond that holds each created thing in relation to every other thing. Like rivers in the blue splash of a word.

Jim and I ease into our goodbyes in the twilight warmth of Burgos. We stand within the hum of the old city walls, beneath an eight-pointed star vaulting the heavens inside the cathedral. The stone arches are smooth and curved like muscles. Those who still worship on bended knee do so in a chapel dedicated to the Santo Cristo, where the carved-out wooden image of a man found at sea has been placed against the wall behind the altar. Enfolded by bovine skin, the image poses in the form of crucifixion, enshrined, hands and feet nailed. His natural hair and fingernails still grow and are clipped in sacred ritual. Beneath his green garment is the scar in his side and the fallow penis. His blood is used to mark doorways where a devil may not enter. People bow and rise, rise and bow, conjuring an inner state of being that stills the heart.

As a final gesture we meander the old city, deep into its centre. Music opens throughout the streets, echoes off stone walls. A quintet of young men play "Pachelbel's Canon" in the Plaza Mayor, then drift into that familiar Mozart, that dah, dah-dah, da-da-da-da-dah. Children laugh and play tag and duck beneath tabletops outside cafés. Those at tables with beer or wine or sweets involve themselves in another kind of worship. Jim strums his guitar in rhythm with the night skies and the quiet of the Arlanzon River. There is pulse and leap in our embrace. So long for now.

All roads must be tested in solitude, a soil-oath to their becoming.

I've been on my own for a week, walking the autumnal heat of these *mesetas* and forty days in an hour's reach. In the low brim shade of my straw hat there's little room to look back. No rain to sustain my cup. Every now and then a branch at my feet offers direction. Or a purpling sunflower with its stigma of death. Then nothing but an open road and still more *mesetas* flanked by pillars of faded wheat which have supported better years. Everything here is marked to live and die. Burgos to Castrojeriz, Fromista to Sahagun, toward León. The road cuts through the ruins of the monastery of San Anton where a farmer has set up barbed wire fences and a warning sign, "Keep back." A dog barks from behind a fence, teeth with a hook. Sheep huddle in their last days. No time for bells or grief. Beneath an archway, a cubbyhole in a wall, where monks once left jugs of fresh water for the passing pilgrim, has been bricked up. There's little to devote oneself to but dry aqueducts, roads excommunicated from rivers, and horizons delicate as a line drawn by a fine pencil.

This earth in its singed quietude and the quietude of my flesh. Midnight without envy and my sleep between the thighs of a red ridge. What surfaces in each dream is wide as the light cast by the moon between villages.

I cross bridges whose cobblestone has been carved and charted by Romans and Crusaders, by unrequited love and wars called holy. Men of armour and men of loss, buried hip to hip. This path lined with broken vows. I pass through villages without train tracks or paved roads, in half darkness. Can only trust in dust. Sundials did not survive the Crusades. I find a small pocket of shade, I crouch in a forest of twelve trees. There's a well with a rope that has been knotted seven times and a bucket with dents and a hole with which the sunlight conspires. I pull the rope and bucket up quickly, avoiding my reflection, and caress the spilling water in my hands. Small puddles at my feet.

I walk without reward or wealth, passing hidden corridors where once bishops and kings swapped faith for swords, silver for lives. It's six hours of skeletal skies and the slap of the road in the bend of each step. Where is there reverence and worship and the bread of belonging? What's that I catch out of the corner of my eye? The disrobing of the infinite? The enchantment of the meseta? I just can't spell it out. But my thinking slows. And more often than not I find myself on my knees, shimmering in the uncertainty.

This Spanish soil. This affair of body and soul. This map of the heart fraught with second and third glances, with looking away. Years of neglect and detour and sorrow, lovers and thieves, pain and rapture grinding and suffering over the things in life I identify with as mine, as me. After years of looking away, I look again, into the sober eyes of a presence in my heart that has always been here. It's love at fourth sight.

I bathe in the porous black membrane of these unploughed fields, in the peeling gleam and crack of the sunflower seed. I live and die with every breath, held in the arms of this grass, against the belly of soil and sun. Suffering is not the problem, no. It's not wanting to suffer that drains us of the deeper life. I'd choose this life and all its love and suffering a thousand times over, just for this moment.

I step through Terradillos de los Templarios, early morning. It's a dirty town of adobe homes and bandaged doorways. A mangy dog drags her tits through dried cow shit. Her mongrel-lover is at the curb, three legs and a black patch over his eye, tongue scrubbing the rim of a broken rum bottle. There's nothing stirring in the eye. A colony of ants busy themselves with the only bone in town. Sparrows dip above red-tiled roofs, in and out of cracked windowpanes. There's nothing more but a horizon too far to spit at and a lone road leading to the village cemetery.

Father, I arrive in Sahagun out of the deep goodbye of my last step. Aging men and women stand out front of their homes, or sit on wooden chairs, leaning back against smooth, worked adobe walls. They sit between sun and shade, beneath hand-cut flowers on windowsills. Near rivers, near trees. The generations of dipping hands and streaming voices.

Father, where are you now? The aging father I will never know? Is that you I see there in the man with the Christmas-coloured sweater, his bent posture? How is it, when you were painting, I learned to read the angle of your back? I learned when to speak, when to hold my tongue. What I'd give just for a moment's conversation now, the North Star of your mind.

After Mother's death, you never did take on another lover, did you? You began surrendering to your own soli-tude, your own thin lines. You learned to love in the invis-ible realm, something in your face undetectable in a mirror. The Sabbath became your lover. You moved deeper into the unseen, spilling yourself. Father, can you ever forgive me? What did I overhear you share with Elle one night at the kitchen table in your studio: how love works through our bodies like the caterpillar as it endeavours to become the monarch butterfly. The four generations of deaths and births this process requires, from caterpillar to butterfly, while making the seasonal migration from Ontario to Northern Mexico, and back, months apart. Years of avoiding the great groundwork of grief, you said, as if you were the butterfly ignoring the work of the caterpillar, the generations of living and dying, the almost moment to moment transformation it requires to move into the wholeness of love. Years, you said, just to find the words for this process within yourself. Just to forgive yourself and bow to the caterpillar's work.

In the thin, slow lines of my own face I see you, Father. The realized process of being and becoming, turned inside out. Forgiveness made flesh.

Between El Burgo Ranero and Mansilla de las Mulas, in a land with less than one hundred trees, men gather in fields, in unbroken circles round the grain of the day. Farmer-priests fingering future hosts. The grain is small and dry, soft as a handful but hard as a single bead. Not yet tender or transmuted, not yet baptized and named Maria or Jose or Jesus. Whose body will it become?

León. A beggar man with sunglasses and cowboy hat sticks out his tongue as I pass through the inner-city walls, Roman conceptions erected on a day of no moon. The streets narrow and slow my steps. It's a city of intricate chapels and cobblestone curves, a pilgrimage within a pilgrimage. A city whose energy takes me by the hand. I enter the cathedral with over eighteen hundred square metres of stained glass, an enormous space built in the form of a Latin cross, worked by twelve hundred years of crimson winds. Morning light makes its way inside the cathedral, soaks the space, then spills out the western doors. I step through wide, resplendent dollops of blue-and-rose stained glass light, feel bathed from the ground up, feel my skeleton ripen.

I angle through the slender streets and pass the open doors of San Isidoro. I step inside the chapel where the perpetual flame of the Blessed Sacrament is allowed to burn through days and nights to the twenty-four-hour watch of pilgrims and canons. The sun rises and sets on the altar. I sit and meditate upon the Sabbath with Jesus the Nazareno in the afternoon of his love. Then, walking west, on the edge of León, there's one last chapel to attend, San Marcos. Tradition has it that the pilgrim should lay themselves face down before the altar and offer up their petitions and aspirations, the three prayers of their heart and faith.

I pray: To suffer wisely. To leave room at the table top for that which I do not know. Ana.

Stepping back outside, there is agency in my heart and step. A sovereign being. The sun sets over the mountains west of León like an orange slice dipped in honey.

Each night my sleep is deep. Pure, serene, without suffering. Then, I don't know how or when, but a dream stirs, an image arises, and thought takes shape. I open my eyes and the world is in bloom.

The rivers I cross and as many battles mark the way. The stories of knights and kings and queens and lovers and pilgrims are depicted on sacred cups or along the sides of bridges.

Dr. Carsten Wolf is on his hands and knees. His black fedora is tilted back, his army fatigues musty and worn. His face is a well-thumbed book. He kneels and crawls, while investigating the ancient walls and arches that buffer and support the most famous bridge on the road to Santiago, crossing the river Orbigo. The bridge and its myriad arches span the centuries, a trade route since Roman times. I join Dr. Wolf on my hands and knees, attracted by his diligence. He shakes my hand, peering at me and introducing himself: historian, professor, just down from Oxford, a lover of bespoken dusts.

It's the story of the bridge's greatest knight, Don Suero de Quinones, that Dr. Wolf is tracing, fingers now moving over two stone monoliths placed in the centre of the bridge, one to each side.

"It was the Holy Year 1434," Dr. Wolf says, a hand on my shoulder, a soft, red dust leaving its imprint. "You understand, whenever the feast of Santiago, July twenty-fifth, falls on a Sunday, that is a Holy Year. Now de Quinones was a young man, a gallant man, ready to lay his life down for his God and faith. But it was the love of a woman which shaped his battles, a scornful woman, it is said, who did not return his love."

Dr. Wolf smiles, standing now and stretching his back. He offers a hand and pulls me to my feet.

"But de Quinones, you understand, was a knight and, well, what could he do? He proposes marriage to the woman of his heart and she hands down an emphatic No. So, what does de Quinones do? He promises a series of firelight jousts, right here on the bridge, right where we are standing, imagine that. He'll defend this passage, this bridge for the pilgrim, in many jousting tournaments, challenging knights from all over Europe to come and fight. Look at these images," Dr. Wolf points out. "De Quinones teams up with nine other knights and vows three hundred lances, to be used and broken in her name, over thirty days of battle. All this to save his heart and honour and hurt, but then, a change of heart, perhaps? Look, having successfully defended the bridge, he makes his way to Santiago in order to give thanks to the Apostle responsible for this road, this sacred way, you see? I'm thinking he must have experienced a conversion of sorts, or gratitude, or at the very least a form of alleviation, because later he returned and offered to protect the pilgrim, like yourself, from roaming thieves. You understand how dangerous the walk was back then, how terror-filled. Spain was once thick with forests and vast distances in which the pilgrim was vulnerable to attack."

"And the woman he loved?" I ask.

"Leonor Toval?"

"Well, did he get the girl in the end?"

"Ah, my pilgrim friend." Dr. Wolf smiles, lifting back his fedora and dusting himself off. "Like most of us spurned by love, he eventually met someone else. Someone for whom he did not have to break three hundred lances."

Now the river Orbigo passes without blood or battle. The bridge spans its hidden phrase like a strand of hair across the wrist. Years of drought and industrialization have altered the river's course. I pass over its defenceless flow with my head down.

My walking now seeps into my flesh as the lapping of night into day. I rise each morning as if from a well, stirred by those who have passed before me. I walk this earth, gathering in what is near and what is distant, along the intimate fold of furrow and road. I peel away precision and planned arrivals, timetables, and name cards. The not knowing where I will be in an hour's time. Father's ashes warm the hearth beneath my tongue. I have inhaled and cherished, lost and wept for the dead who become me the more I love and honour them. What I imagined would fade with time has shot up through my breast one hundredfold.

It's been three days of shrinking villages and the gloried ruins of stone homes and farmsteads, Old World monasteries and the secularization of smoke. I pass through Astorga and pick up provisions for the way ahead. Mountains, I'm told. Monte Irago. Be prepared. In Santa Catalina de Somoza the bells still ring for Sunday Mass. In a small church dedicated to the relic remains of a San Blas, three elderly women attend. There's an altar boy who stands with arms folded, legs apart, a firm jaw, like a bouncer guarding a nightclub. The village priest leans a little to his right, has the look of someone who has presided over more funerals than weddings and births. At times he forgets himself and everyone else, and celebrates Mass only to keep the bread and wine for himself, scurrying into the sacristy, taking with him sustenance to last the week. When I knock on the sacristy door I hear furniture being dragged across the stone floor toward the door, a barricade of fear. The altar boy takes me by the arm and shows me the way out. The three women cross themselves, go bended through the doors, and lock up the church. A crisis of communion swells in the throats of dry fonts.

Rabanal is a village built on a sharp incline, its main thoroughfare is so steep and uneven that my knees knock up against my chest as I climb. The road is all chipped cobble-stone and chunks of boulder sticking up and out like broken teeth. Impossible for a vehicle to pass. I step from rock to boulder, up the steep terrain, my walking stick leading the way. The roadside homes are small and stone-dark and exposed to the mountain elements of mist and rain that are in constant flow, waving overhead like sheets on a line. I stop here because my breath needs recompense and my legs have had enough. I sit inside the only tavern in town, a wormhole carved out of wood and stone. I'm served up a thick garlic soup, a board of meats and cheeses and bread, and a wine so dark and bold and red, each sip stirs the soul. I listen to the men and women and their late Sunday afternoon talk, sports and politics; the Communists and old Fascists and Social Democrats and Christian Democrats straining through their cups of drunken order, through abandoned creeds and holy water lifted from the local church, the quiet ruins of Santa Maria. Here in this town they celebrate the liberation of the human spirit with that awkward dance of one step up the hill, two steps back down. I'm given a cot in a backroom, next to a glassless window where the cool night mists enter and settle on my brow.

I stand on the eastern slope of Monte Irago and look back over the long morning lowlands surrounding León, through which I've walked, and then forward into the riding heights and snow-kissed ridges known to the Romans in their days of conquest as the Mountains of Mercury. Up there, as a testament to their god of quicksilver and eloquence, they erected an iron cross. The Cruz de Ferro. The cross sits atop a five-metre oak pole that stands against the heights, part beacon, part slash against sky. At an altitude of almost fifteen hundred metres. The pole is surrounded by a thick pile of dusted rocks and stones that have been placed at its base, one by one, by pilgrims of the way. A rite of passage, the stones were carried up the hill from Foncebadón, along the winding road, its sharp traverse. Prayer stones which, when rubbed, give off a spark of unconditional light. Prayer stones that say, "I am here, and I have been here a thousand years, waiting for you. If you are lonely and lost, lean into me, and I will show you a way through."

Foncebadón is a ruin of blue-grey slate roofs and rotting wood beams, shattered windows overlooking a valley precipice to the south, and a single bell tower through which the cold north winds pass. Morning light sifts through the abandoned village, as if combing back the hair of a corpse. Was it the winds that chased the inhabitants away, or a random demise; war or rumours of war, marauding tribes, the Crusaders and the Moors, or the village well having lost its inner power? . . . so many stories of abandon circle the village. The sky falls here as if into the point of a spear. Great birds of prey hover without moving their wings.

It's here I must palm my sacred stone and gather up my secret prayers. I must climb and pass through the many shadow-events I've sheltered along the way and the seventy lives of the forgiving heart. This path that is illuminated by a light which has travelled a million solar systems to reach me at the ends of my fingertips. When I place my prayer stone at the foot of the iron cross, in the congregation of a million other stones, I find my hands running the length of my body, divining places of water and wounding, well-springs where my mind dips. What is hidden and yearning is lifted into the soft sheen of a midday sun. I hear the voice of my prayer stone, whispering down through the generations: *Lean into me, Pilgrim. I am here for you and will be for a thousand years to come.*

Life beyond the iron cross. I step into the cool heights and further peaks worked by lightning storms and great arcs of weather. A man in a house on a hill rings a bell for each passing pilgrim. I follow the sun's flashing halo through thin cloud cover, on rock. Silence multiplies in my hands like the five loaves of bread Jesus once offered and wept over, the extent of his love.

I rest on a peak rock before the descent into Acebo. Sweating, I bundle up to avoid a chill. My stomach growls. Alto Altar at 1,515 metres. The air is pure and poised and close. Above me is the sun. A funnel of clouds pour in from the west, filling the valley below with a light rain. The valley seems to move in and out with my breath. More clouds funnel in, pouring themselves into the valley, leaving the gift of rain. The valley is receptive and becomes a bowl, holding the contents of moisture left by the clouds. I fall into a trance and this utter felt-tone of pouring and receiving, receiving and pouring, until all in one breath it seems that the whole of the sky and clouds and rain is contained in that simple and singular valley bowl, and everything suddenly stops and goes dark as deep dreamless sleep, and all that I think I am and the world to be, all I've identified with, is gone. Then, out of the quiet blackness of sleep, the valley heaves and breathes out, pouring its wild contents of sky and cloud and moisture back up into an opening which becomes sky and cloud and rain again, and then flows on, passing over. How is it I can be lost and found in a single breath? How is it that all along the Universe has been awake to itself in me?

This is why the ancients taught not to say God's name.

I descend the mountain without a word. Only the worked-in sound of my boots over stone and road and gravel path. The light rain has passed, the sun warming over my shoulder. The way twists through open mountain passes, switchbacks, quick turns, the road falling off into forest ravines and back up along narrow cliffs and back down again. I keep an eye on each foot, how I place it and where I step. The descent is hard on my knees. I pass through Acebo, glancing and nodding as I walk. As hard as the descent is, I am flooded with gratitude. I don't stop until Molinaseca. I cross the bridge into town and go down to the river and wash my face and neck in the cool Meruelo until every one of my pores stir.

Ana, with each step and river crossing I enter the slow orbit of our return, pressing nearer our prayer and sex. Your extraordinary stillness and touch. The river-erotics of our tongues.

I sleep the night in an abandoned barn, curled up on the upper floorboards like a cat.

For three or four days I walk the lowlands flowing out of the heights of Monte Irago. I ease into step with field after field of autumnal vineyards flush with the last of a day's sun. A sense of rust to the season. The harvest has passed. Molinaseca to Ponferrada, Cacabelos to Villafranca del Bierzo. In an oak forest dedicated to an apparition of the Virgin Mary, I stand with the great limbs of holm oak which cause my arms to lift a little through the whisper and pull of five-hundred-year-old bark. There is clarity of will, heart, and mind at the touch of dusk. I say goodbye to that which no longer serves the greater good.

Father learned to look for the emergent in his art. A realized property that neither his brush nor the canvas nor himself or his subject could bring forth on their own. They required relationship, a synergistic interplay. The way the heart made up of heart cells can pump blood but the cells on their own cannot. Synergy is an art within an art within an art, Father held. He sometimes lovingly referred to me as Emergent Wonder. A unique being neither he nor Mother could create as individuals, I was the emergent child made in the fullness and wonder of their love.

A farmer named Miguel Jose Corpas surprises me on the road. He takes me by the elbow as I pass and guides me to a table and two chairs set beneath fruit trees and vines: fig, apple, grape. A man in his sixties, he's solid and soiled and earthed. A sweet, weathered face, lines like those of wood carved by wind. On the tabletop is a jug of wine, slices of fruit, cheese, Galician bread as large as the heart of a mythical creature, and a wooden plate with fresh octopi. Cooked to intimate taste in a blackened cauldron off to the side of the road, the octopi glimmer in a steaming bath, their red-flecked flesh becoming almost see-through. The octopi are cut into small ringlets, like cedar knots. I'm invited to select my ringlet with a toothpick, lift it dripping with olive oil, vinegar, salt, paprika, cayenne pepper, and slip the piece between my lips.

A minute of food and conversation with Miguel becomes an hour, an hour a day, and I end up staying the night and then another day and then two. I help Miguel with his work. Simple tasks, gathering hay and grass, feeding cows, tending sheep, cleaning the pigpen, pruning vines, cutting grapes into clusters for the year's new wine. Sun-up to sundown. In the late afternoon we spend an hour lifting and removing rocks from a barren black field that has been left fallow for a year. I can't walk over the field without feeling myself sink a little, searching for my balance while heaving the rocks into the back-end loader attached to the tractor. Miguel's son Pedro drives the tractor off to the side of the field and dumps the rocks in one large pile. Miguel and I wipe our brows and look to the sky.

Miguel worries that the way of the local farmer is in jeopardy. He senses global forces are moving in, agribusiness pinching up land and homes as it goes, announcing monoculture as the way, the truth, and life. The land we stand on is the fruit of generations of work. But it's not just this work, he tells me, but the work of cows and their dung, sheep, pigs, horses, and the work of worms. Not to mention the things we cannot see, he points out. Enzymes and molecules and bacteria. Things so small it's a wonder they have a name.

"It's not enough to just look at the earth," Miguel says, trimming his vision. "It's not enough to take in her vistas and views and obvious beauty. You must taste her, roll in her, sleep with her, to know her genius, her faithfulness."

Miguel bends down to the soil and invites me to join him. He sifts a hand through the moist, curling furrows between us, combing their fallow folds. He scoops up a handful of topsoil, packing it tight in his palm. He adds his spittle, working the soil into a patty, shaping it, then holding out the glittering concoction.

"Is there anything you'd like to add?" he asks, looking me in the eyes.

I pause, roll with the moment, then lift a pinch of Father's ashes from the leather medicine pouch and rub them into Miguel's miracle of matter and play.

"Take a bite," he says.

I don't know if it's the earth's own genius or the humility of Miguel's work and touch I taste, but something of the soil's rippling cursive flows over my tongue and moves down my throat as through old cave dwellings, educing in my chest the fires and winds of a first expression of night faith. Life belongs to the generosity of the invisible world, as in the way two people love.

Elle, I know a place now of earth that takes pleasure in making peace between what we call the spiritual life and my flesh. Through you, a light and a heat that are alive.

I enter the Valcarce River valley system beyond Villafranca and immediately sink in awe. Fully primed, Miguel has provided for the way. Wrapped meats and cheeses and bread and full wine skin. I decide on slowness as I walk. The climate is wild and moist and changes in a mood's nod. Clouds stream in and stream out, leaving their bright mark of rain. Then the sun breaks through and licks up every drop of moisture from the road and my back. I take the route to Alto Pradela, a steep, 1,200-metre intrusion into the Valcarce hillside, winding through a thick wooded outcrop of pine and chestnut trees. Every corner of my lungs and breath are required for both the climb and the descent. Seven hours and 20K. I've been fortunate to receive so many teachers along the way, none more authentic than the current step. I arrive in Vega de Valcarce soaked to the bone after a quick thunder shower sent a shudder through the valley. Not even my poncho could hold back the stealth of storm. I'm given space in a beaten-up hostel for pilgrims. A young boy shows me in. An old four-room schoolhouse, a door that won't close, sixteen bunk beds, and two broken windows, glass across the floor. The shower is cold. A local woman arrives and apologizes for the mess. She's not sure about the broken glass, what happened. She holds a hand to her heart and shakes her head. An elder, she indicates she's been begging local authorities to build a proper hostel for pilgrims. She leaves and returns with a broom and dustbin and a bowl of *caldo gallego*, a succulent meat and vegetable soup. I warm myself up with the soup, then by helping sweep up the glass and dust and hang my damp clothing on a makeshift line from wall to wall. The elder, Rosalia, says good evening and bows out the door. She promises coffee and bread and jam in the morning. Six a.m. I sleep away the night next to the rush and call of the river. Tomorrow is another climb.

Here it is. The climb to O Cebreiro. All along the way people have mentioned it, as if it holds its own tale of passion and myth. As if to experience its essential nature is to be stripped of everything but God's very essence. Face to face, eye to eye, with the Maker.

The climb is a slow seduction. First, the river valley lures me back in, the Valcarce rushing strong and sweet and clear as I walk with it toward Las Herrerías. The land is lush and black-green and wet, womblike and dark. Morning mists drape themselves over primitive trees. Droplets of water in the air smooth my brow. The air is crisp and naked. I fall in love. In quiet, wet pastures sheep roam, their bells ringing, geese and chickens following in morning stride. I step over cow dung in the road. A lone man walks, dog in tow, stick in hand, nudging a thick, black stallion, balls swinging. I wander through Las Herrerías, following the river as it narrows. From a home a solo line of smoke and the smell of bread. Come hither, I hear. Then the ascent shows its legs.

I enter the blistering climb, step into a valley floor, then quickly up along a thin slope covered in rocks and boulders and mud, yesterday's rain, shit, and runoff. A pathway for oxen, pilgrims, and goats. My footsteps negotiate the worn spaces between bleached stones embedded beneath the surface of the muddy earth. I borrow the muscle of rock and stone and hop from one to the other. The air is potent with late October. It is silent. I follow the fading chestnut trees lined up and around the heavy switchbacks of mountain path. The sky is hidden. A cow pokes her head through a barbed wire fence, stares me down. Her powerful breath releases into the air. The slope she stands on fills me with a sense that we're actually falling back down the path through mud and rock and dung. I turn my focus back to the ground at hand. One more step and turn and I find myself in a space of open air, a mist pulling across a slanting field of opulent green. I pause, feel the root of my breath. Across the field a mountain horizon seems to call. *Nothing*, I think, *nothing is wasted on the soul.*

Sweat works its way across my back and brow. I rest by a fountain in the hamlet of La Faba and look back over the treetops giving cover to the Valcarce valley. Such stillness here as to shatter every thought otherwise. I fill my water bottle and take a slow sip. If our speech is holy and the names we give are holy, every word is holy. I must become a wise virtuoso in what I say and how I say it.

Back into the climb, more chestnut trees, more mist and mud and road. The easy repetition becomes beautiful, like listening to a favourite song over and over, getting into its groove. A farmer is walking downhill from Laguna de Castilla, twenty or so cows trailing with him on the narrow path. Heads, tails, large bodies swaying to the rhythm of bells. I move upstream into their song and current, passing a hand along their shoulders and backs. The farmer nods. A few more K, a stroll through Laguna, and I break out into the land of Galicia, its rolling mists and heights. I stop and gaze. This land of primitive streams and wild, uneven pastures accentuated by muscular, criss-crossing roads, stone walls, and ruins. Small villages nestle in intimate valleys. Smoke. Archaeologists arrive and gasp: to dig would be a sin. It's a land Original and Celtic and Roman and Biblical and Big Bang. It holds dark temples of childhood secrets. Flower patterns of laughter inside the ear. A kiss from the lips of now.

O Cebreiro is a village that sits on a peak as in the palm of an outstretched hand. Like the man in the fourteenth-century miracle story, I've made the slow, ponderous 8K climb to hear Mass. In the story, a peasant from a distant village navigated his way here through the wash and trembling of a fantastic snowstorm, each step a sacred gesture toward the church of Santa María la Real. A priest whose faith was waning celebrated the Mass, and inwardly scolded the peasant for coming to church through such a storm. The peasant was out of breath, soaked through, and took his place in the pew. Then, as the priest intoned the Mass, weaving its spell of incense and candlelight, at the moment of offering the bread and the wine to the peasant, something happened. The bread changed to real flesh and the wine to real blood. The priest recoiled, eyes forced apart. It's impossible now to pass through this village without taking on an aspect of its story, whether it be in the form of the silent glow of the miracle chalice or in the gentle spin of faith from the peasant's wet step, his winemaker's press.

What is it to destroy a temple and to rebuild it in three days? I wait a lifetime in the Jerusalem of my heart, I wait through social and political movements, cataclysms of the soul, each wound and border crossing. I wait until suddenly my faith is realized in the moment between picking a grape and cradling it upon my tongue, tasting the delicate symbiosis between two worlds of skin, one of grape, the other of flesh. All those philosophical arguments which seemed to matter so much come down now to this; the sanctity of experience just as it is.

I rest through the night in one of nine prehistoric huts that dot the peak of O Cebreiro. The huts are called *pallozas.* Low, dank earthen structures. Thatched roofs of straw and reed. Small windows and doorways framed with stone. The interior walls have been cooked and blackened by centuries of home fires and smoke. Refuge for the modern-day pilgrim, I sleep in this strange, intoxicating place with an eye toward what matters. To love without having to hoard the fire's warmth for oneself. To love without having to turn one's back on one's call. To serve this love through the three water wheels of love: God, neighbour, self. Only in the inpouring and outpouring of love, round and round, one into the other, are we enhanced by what has been received and what there is to give.

Days and nights of sandpaper rain. I wander Galicia's valley worlds, second and third order climbs and descents. Triacastela to Sarrià and beyond. Galicia's pine and eucalyptus forests are ample, sweet, and succulent. Now and then the sun tips its hat to her freehanded curves. Roosters strut and celebrate the way. I pass an *ermita*, Our Lady of the Snows. A few wooden benches within its crooked structure. A priest's robes hang from a rafter, brushing the altar with its green hem. A single candle burns. There are many ways to remain in prayer.

I cross the dam and reservoir of Portomarín where, beneath the charged waters, the ancient settlement of the village still stirs, submerged and saturated with its gone history, gleaming like a petrified jewel. It stares up at the passing pilgrim as if from behind the eye sockets of a saint's skull. The new Portomarín straddles the crest of the hill overlooking the dam and reservoir. Only the church of the original settlement remains, having been moved stone by stone up the hill, each stone marked with a number to indicate its time and place.

I walk without urgency, buffered by the tributaries of each step. I pass milestones which spell out how far I've come, how far I've yet to go. The numbers no longer matter and perhaps never did. To what end have I been walking, travelling, drifting? I've released Father's ashes over the earth, in the sea rush and anointment of every arrival and parting. What more is there for me to reconcile but the confluence of my own death with a time and place I do not know, where my body, its million tiny bones like broken stems or pick-up sticks, or as ashes and the random sowing of seed, will be scattered, sprinkled, and delivered back across the pathways of earth and years. From whose hands I might be blessed and spread, I don't know. There is peace in not knowing. I imagine my children, a son or a daughter as woodcutters chipping into their own journeys, collecting my pale remains and flashing them over a garden. To mingle with the data of limestone and dark matter. Perhaps a new species of plant or flower to emerge.

There are a handful of us now, walkers of the way. Mick, D. Trujillo, Ava, and Juan from down under Argentina. We stream toward Santiago. We move in and out of one another's lives for a few days, pausing with views, swapping food and stories and body aches. At night there are meals around tabletops and mutual snoring from atop bunk beds. In Melide we stop at noon on a Sunday and feast on *pulpo* in a garage-style restaurant, half a football stadium in size. Large wooden tables, locals upon locals, octopi served on wooden plates; potatoes and salad and jugs of wine. Then we walk on, true to our pace and word.

There is something in our lives unfolding west. Energies that journey in a bird call or a child's hand at play. Each of my footsteps first rise, then bow. Santiago sets its seal upon my heart like an ineffable verse, like a birthmark on the sun.

I move up the road from Lavacolla toward Monte do Gozo, the Mountain of Joy. It's from here I first see the holy city, its red-crested undertones of granite and slate, with an intimacy that surprises. How many millions of footsteps has it taken for me to arrive, how many times have I faltered or knelt, unable to turn back? I witness the grandeur of Santiago from a distance of five kilometres. The city and its enfolding landscapes are far removed from Van Gogh's place of art and wounding, but his words travel. *My own work, I am risking my life for it and my reason has half foundered.*

I collapse back onto the earth in a heap of praise.

I slip across the crest of Monte do Gozo, my walking stick leading the way. My legs lift as through ancient maps known for their errors of scale and power. Beneath my footprints a reign of living organisms thrive. My life resembles a missing page from a holy book, now found and re-bound. The revelations of emotions, sacred moods. I've learned to make wine from a broken heart. I look down through the suburbs of the city into the inlets of its modernization, over paved roads and highways, until there, against a green-black backdrop of further mountains and sunsets, I see the cathedral, its three spiralling towers above a city of forty churches. Bells announce the unreachable reached. Ana, the peace I feel here is as with my ear upon your shell-like belly.

I hold the vision of the city, my heart in tune. I turn and plant my walking stick in the earth. It has delivered me well. The acorn becomes an oak.

It's a five-kilometre walk from Monte do Gozo, down stone and pebble roads, over the highways, through the ringed streets, to the cathedral. In ancient times the last of the walk was made barefoot. I make a smudge of Father's ashes over the soles of my feet.

The inner city has been bathed in morning rain but the sun works its way through cloud cover. I'm guided now by everything that has gone on ahead of me, grace unseen. I walk through Plaza de Cervantes, a place without cars or horns, traffic signals, or the need for police. Locals go about the routines of their daily lives. Heaven glitters in the rain-soaked cobblestone, a golden tinge. Men in old black fedoras and women in dresses seized by autumn. A stick of bread protrudes from a shopping bag. It's a city of students and priests in dark cassocks, fountains and markets leading the way.

I walk past the Via Sacra, in the shadow of the cathedral, its holy entrance hidden from first view. I walk beneath an archway where a man is playing Galician bagpipes, his body still, his tune announcing the pilgrim. I pause and listen, then step down the worn granite steps, and land in Plaza del Obradoiro. I gaze into the simple immensity of the plaza and feel the pleasure of my arrival in its swift narrative of rain, mist, song, and sun, the pilgrim's tools. Now my feet, bare and awake, seem to know the way. A handful of paces and I find myself anchored in the centre of the plaza, dazzled, and turning to face the cathedral. Love seems truer, now that I can't explain why.

In the dark blue-green gaze of the cathedral's entrance, I spot the Pórtico de la Gloria, last opening without disguise. My next step arises from a full heart.

There's a marble pillar inside the entrance, thick as an old oak tree. The Tree of Jesse, it supports a sacred story shaped in stone. There's Jesus in his loving prime, flanked by his fishermen companions, arching over the great doors.

Carved beneath Jesus is his brother, Santiago. He sits on the pillar and welcomes the pilgrim, receiving their prayers and sending them off on their own journeys. At his feet, pressed into the base of the marble trunk, are the finger holes I'm invited to touch. The holes have been worked into the marble over the centuries by the thousands upon thousands of pilgrims who have come and gone, sinking their finger-tips and the palm of their hand into the stone, loosening its insides. I become a sculptor who lends my touch, bows my head, and kisses the foot of the pillar, while giving thanks on a day of both sun and rain. My hand at a confluence, sinking into marble, into the fourteen billion years of waves and bloom and starlit roads.

Inside the cathedral, I sit with the mythic contours of its history. Floors groomed by Celtic mists. Roman occupa-tions. Stone converted by Christian myth. Other gods and goddesses' rivalry. I sit with the story of a gentle fisherman from Galilee, Santiago—James, Jacques, Iago, Jacobi, Giacome. His martyred body which was transported here from the holy land, by stone boat, by disciples of the faith and the underground. His burial here at the extreme edge of the Old World, far from the hands of those looking the other way. Until the night the shepherd witnessed that star falling in the valley system surrounding the old city, a star falling on a field of graves. *Compostela*, the field of the stars.

So this walk with the stars. This walk to remember a life conceived before I had been given a name, before separation and loss and fatigue. This walk soaked in the Milky Way. From stardust to the Sermon on the Mount, so many daring, evolutionary steps have arisen. As many steps as there are stars in the sky. I've risked but a few. Whatever the nuanced reasons for arriving here—to touch the pillar, to embrace the Apostle's statue, to forgive the perilous nature of history, my own fault lines and the black ice that first tripped me up—my life has shifted, like the wind out of the west. Like the magician who pulls the tablecloth out from under cutlery and china and glasses full of wine, and somehow, through deftness and wit, leaves everything standing in place on the tabletop. Here, yes here, I'm standing. It's as miraculous as the blood coursing my veins. For however long I remain here, contemplating the massive spaces, the wafts of incense and the scent of perspiration clinging to the faithful, I see my arrival is not permanent. No matter how long I'd like each embrace to last, there will be other, unknown steps. The heart will play again. There will be fruit to peel, and love's invocatory rite. So my body roams its seasons of ancient faith, and enters the darkness where my breath must calculate the intent of further stars and the road.

I move up behind the grand altar and find the Apostle's statue. I stand in silence before this strange skeletal and bejewelled form, then move my arms around its great golden shoulders, giving my hug. My awkward limbs, my awkward faith. I remember all the mentors of embrace who have encouraged me this far, the guides of touch and care and word, the dead and the alive, so many loving souls, their arms and hands around me, delicate as feathers shed and gathered to line a nest.

Thank you . . . *Gracias* . . . *Merci*.

Now, how might I serve these many gifts.

For three days and nights I settle into the city. I wander its public squares, its café life, its celebratory appeal. I find Mick and D. Trujillo at the Benedictine seminary where we are all staying. Together we stroll the narrow streets of the old city and feast on tapas, wine, and local dishes deep into the mornings. Galician music—bagpipes and flutes and guitar—is piped into the city, spills from gift shops, or live from the hands and mouths of small groups of students, modern-day troubadours. Markets gleam with fresh fish, fruit, hand-cut flowers, bread, still warm and rising at one's touch. We step in and out of small, dark churches, in and out of the cathedral, always filled with people busy in prayer, women with bright rosary beads, priests and pilgrims weaving closer to massive altars from which colourful saints and angels lean and peer, whispering of their lives and lessons. At noon each day there is a Mass for pilgrims as they arrive step by step, processing through the Pórtico de la Gloria, tired, unwashed, and ecstatic. The nationality of the previous day's arrivals and their starting points on the road to Santiago are read aloud. Irish/Chartres. Canadian/Le Puy. American/Pamplona. Into the Mass the organ sounds off, builds in reverent tempo, goes base deep and sends a tremor of notes through the congregation. Soul-nerves quiver and leap and rejoice. The Botafumeiro, a huge thurible ripe with incense, swings from transept to transept, guided by eight red-robed men holding down a thick braided rope which is wound round a mechanical pulley system set high in the central cupola. The smell of incense floods the cathedral, bathing us all. I find myself standing in the pews, swaying with the censor. I close my eyes. Between notes of grace I inhale a silence which has become radiant. World within and world without. God is in the breath.

FINISTERRE

It's just under a week's walk from Santiago to the end of the earth. Finisterre. A wild, unrelenting place of salt and thirst. A huge body of water, an endless sky, the moody horizons. All of Creation seems to unfurl here. There are wandering mists, down on all fours; tongues of cloud working against a thick storm-swept coastline. Crooked, blood-tinged cliffs, slopes, edges of stone falling into inexhaustible depths. Attached to black rock, the blue mouths of slow-opening mussels play with water, salt, and air, bracing sinew against the intense wave.

This coast of the Atlantic is called the Coast of Death. Roman centurions arrived here and pondered the breadth of their realm and fate beneath a stone cross made smooth and white by the spray of salt and sun. But with no further to advance and no more lands and peoples to conquer, limited by a body of water, what else was there for them to do but to throw themselves into another world of gods and depths and myths. Or to die without cause.

I stand atop the cliffs and soak in the expanse of ocean. Behind me there are hills of pine and seagulls on the wind.

Wild cornstalks grow up and down the side of the cliff. Here, everything slopes, sinks, eventually surrenders. Yet here, at the end of the earth, surrendering comes to me as the first kernel of wisdom. I breathe it in, loosen my hold. The ocean draws me out, fills me with its primal meaning.

There is water coursing my skin that is as ancient as Creation's original, pouring forth. There is water within, and fire again. A brotherhood of stars and salt, a sisterhood of waves and moonlight, running the breadth of my body, unhindered by thought or emotion, sense or feeling, unhooked and flowing.

I step down to the waters, the roaring, quick Atlantic. Waves spill in like giant footholds, muscular, strong-willed currents. I face the gleaming of possibility. I face that aspect of myself not yet born. That aspect of myself, like Father's ashes, I resolve to bestow.

I slip off my clothes.

In November the Atlantic is cold and exacting. I wade into a pool between the jagged cliffs, naked as the blue mussels loosened by wave and sun. Down to the last pinches of Father's ashes, I wet my fingertips and mark myself with his wise remains. I trace four lines from the top of my head, over my brow, down my face, neck, chest, stomach, and genitals. The seven points of praise. I slip into the ocean's pull, feeling the force of an undertow. I dive under and swim out and feel the warm counterglow of something blue-grey and flickering, washing off from my body. Father's ashes stream back toward the surface, setting off; distinct, gone.

I emerge from the brittle waters, my body stinging and alert. I sense how strong and fragile my heartbeat is within my chest, the extraordinary fragility of a lyric which has become mine to voice, forged in the potent fire of grief. Yes. If God is singing a song of creation and I am one word in that great chorus of the Universe, each of us potentiated with our one, unique word to give, what word would I be? Yes, I would be Yes.

II AGAPE

CABBAGETOWN

I'm here at Agape House. It's nestled down here on Ontario Street, south of Carlton. The house is an oasis, a deeper well stirring in a city that is struggling to maintain fertile ground. Toronto. I'm home for the first time in years.

Sebastian. His story surfaces like a gentle wave, a still point upon which I gather words, images, meaning. I first met him five years ago, at the University of Toronto, when I took his course in Religion and Literature. He took me under his wise wing and introduced me to the works of Eckhart and Merton, Dostoevsky, Saint-Exupéry, Dorothy Day, and de Chardin. Now, he's dead on fifty years of age. Dark hair, some curls. Deep brown eyes, serene but intense. His focus is sometimes alarming. There's the two-, three-days' stubble. He moves with ease, never appears late. His transition from one moment to another seems meditative, artful, honed through years of service. He spent most of his childhood south of most known borders, way down there, Chile to be exact. His mother was indigenous to Chile, a teacher; and his father was also a teacher who left Canada for the educational systems of the southern hemisphere with a hope to bring a sense of justice to a land groping to find its just course. Sebastian was fed by his parents love of education and a thirst for justice, and easily moved into his own work: a flare for making connections, mercury-like, sealed by iron in his blood. Talent and effort and the heart and brains, he found himself studying with the Jesuits at the University of El Salvador. There, as an undergrad, he met a woman who stirred his insides. A brief courtship led to a marriage and over a period of five years the birth of three children and their move to a small village where they lived the communal life. Then Sebastian lost it all, save a daughter, to the slaughters of the day, a military raid, the new regime. He doesn't go into details; there is a sense the story is still tender. From there, he says, he descended into a world of loss, while taking on the eternal weight of having to learn how to walk again.

He kept up his studies though, fuelled by a deep need for justice, and the legacy of his parents' embrace. Then, as grace would have it, he heard Oscar Romero on the radio, heard the man talk of change, of liberation, of equality among souls, then he witnessed the change happening. Eventually he met the man with the words. Sebastian did more than shake hands with the man; he studied with man, broke bread with the man. Sebastian came north just before Romero's assassination. He began a year of studies at Regis College, mixing in his master's degree in theology with two unlikely companions at the time, ethics and ecology. Then he began teaching his own course at U of T. But it all changed again, he says, with the death of his mother, followed a month later by the death of his father. His mother died in her sleep and his father withered in her absence, a broken heart getting the better of his sorrow-stricken body.

Those deaths brought to Sebastian a humble inheritance, the unexpected. Years of struggle, Sebastian says, and *Boom!* He claps his hands together once, *Boom!* What to do? he wondered. Here, in a city he suddenly called home. "There's something familiar here," he said. Something in the streets, a struggle he recognized.

He sees the growing gap between rich and poor, the same signs he witnessed in El Salvador; the thirst, the injustice, the disparity. There might not be military oppression here, he says, but there is an oppression of a subtler order; there is the oppression of imagination, an anti-intellectualism, a violence to our way of thinking that is becoming deeply rooted. We are running the risk of believing that we can poison the rivers and lakes and soils, our bodies and minds, and somehow survive.

So, what does Sebastian do with his inheritance? He doesn't travel the world. No. He purchases this grand old structure and opens a Catholic Worker House. Influenced by Dorothy Day and her writings and the Catholic worker movement of the 1930s, he does something right in the heart of the place where he senses the fear to be. He refurbishes, renovates, opens the doors. He goes public without making speeches. He turns the crank counterculture; he actually throws the crank away, gets out a handful of seed and a hoe, and reworks a sense of culture and being as best he can within others' company. A communion of saints.

"I saw the justice we require would most likely not happen through our present political structures or the individual nation state," he shared with me one day after class. "It will come to us only as we learn to see how interdependent we are as a species. We must create spaces not only for the *revolution* of the heart and mind, but a *renaissance* of the heart and mind as well. That begins with foundations, the sober work within ourselves and within the collective; those within our sphere of love and influence. We must ground our hearts in care. We can't expect to take care of a tree's branches and leaves without tending to the soils and roots and trunks. With that, only one other ancient teaching made sense to me: feed the hungry, clothe the naked, shelter the homeless."

I'm welcome to stay as long as I require. Sebastian assures me of this. I explain there's a woman. That she will be joining me in a matter of weeks. That I love her. Want to spend the rest of my days and nights with her. Sebastian eases a hand across my shoulder, insists there's enough space in the house and my room to shelter her as well. He loves stories of the heart. Feasts. Rings.

Ana, I'm in a third-floor room, at the back of the house, out of the way. There are four or five other rooms on the floor, plus a shared washroom. The room is just right for now, a good fit for the two of us. Small, but with space enough for a double bed, a simple desk, an old wooden chair, a night table with a lamp, and the chipped crucifix hanging over the bed. There is a small closet but I don't have many clothes to worry about these days; second-hand stuff, two pairs of jeans, a few T-shirts, two good cotton shirts, a blue sweater, and a winter jacket. I keep socks and underwear in a wooden box under the bed. And I have few pairs of shoes. Hiking boots, picked up in Rome, and a pair of sandals. There's a four-paned window onto the world outside, facing east, down a back alley. Lining the alley and other back-yards are six oak trees, layered with bent limbs, whitened by snow cover, plunging into the earth. There is a sense of the numinous in the oaks' stand, gnarled, ancient, sharing in its shine.

Lent is approaching, my love. The forty days and nights. A time and space to re-attune my heart with the Catholic in me, the universal stuff of blood, breath, bone, night, soul, death, tomb, heaven infusing earth. Home. Yes, it's time to reclaim a place to walk, a field near the curve of a stream. Time to lie there, procumbent, my arms spread, genitals falling forward. Time to exchange with the soils and roots the energies and substances I've received along the way, which make up the world as it is. Glorious.

I'm Catholic, yes. Catholic in the Word making flesh, Catholic in the gutsy and sensuous Universe, Catholic in the resilient ruins of two thousand years, in the archaeological digs and catacombs and cells where the saints' prayers were made, sweated out, perhaps never heard. I'm Catholic in root in river in road, yes. I'm Catholic in the cut betwixt worlds, holding the uncertainty of why. I'm Catholic in erotic gardens and the sacred text of a seed. I'm Catholic in wind, in claw, in ink and scroll. Catholic in streams of blood and semen and menstrual flow. I'm Catholic in you and me and Other and separateness dissolved; in stars unfurling, in the sun compelling this body to stand, these eyes to blink, yes. I'm Catholic in God in process, Catholic in love; Catholic in the reverence of a co-suffering embrace. I'm Catholic with all my clothes off, Catholic while working up a good sweat, growing my beard, spending quality time on my knees, yes. I'm Catholic reaching back a hand. Catholic at 3 a.m. Catholic at the banquet table cobbled out of the banned and the broken and the golden. I'm Catholic beholding the tragic and the beautiful and the sublime embers of unknowing. I'm Catholic in that divine gaze showing through all our expressions. The intimate, the vulnerable, the complex. Yes. I'm Catholic in the dynamic ground of being, dying and becoming, dying and becoming, even though the headstones say otherwise. I'm Catholic in the so-utterly-transcendent that is so-utterly-immanent that my world is constantly being blown open by the wonder and grace of it all. Yes. I'm Catholic all the way up and all the way down. I'm Catholic like a water wheel, pouring and receiving, receiving and pouring, yes. I'm Catholic at the intersection of the crossbeams where that Broken Son's heart like a seed dies into the earth, but dies only to burst into branch and bloom, and the birds of the air come and find shelter in song. Yes. I'm Catholic in that orchestral heart space, learning how to hold the God-note we tune to.

Fourteen billion years and still in the unfolding, yes. Old wine, new wine, I savour the praise.

Aiden is known as the welcome mat here. He's always positioned nearest the front door, sleeps the night on two cushions placed on the floor. Says he's like a cat, always on the alert. He has a long, thin catlike body too, a little curve to the spine, long arms and legs. His eyes are green, almost transparent, tempered as a great leaf drenched in rain. In our short hike down the hall and winding stairs, he gets what he calls the basics of his life out. He hails from south of the border, New England area, Boston. Says he's a Red Sox fan, thus doomed to a certain frustration with life. He talks of the Buckner bounce and the ghost of the Babe as if both were somehow fighting it out in his throat. He fought in the Korean War, was wounded in the left leg, leaving him with a slight limp. Then he took to the wandering life during the early sixties, only to re-emerge mid-decade with the music of Bob Dylan. He witnessed (in person, he says) Berkley, Kent State, even Woodstock in its primal thrust. In the seventies Aiden hunkered down in Colorado and read the greats of his multi-layered ancestry—Emerson, Thoreau, Whitman, his beloved Twain—and worked in various religious communities around the States, a handyman here, a welcome mat there. A few years ago he met Sebastian at a Catholic Worker gathering in Washington. He listened to Sebastian speak about life here in Agape House, liked what he heard, and offered his hand. Sebastian accepted. Aiden spends his time answering the door and providing the first morsel of hospitality to all who knock.

The Welcome Room—a large, renovated space carved out of an old living room and dining room—fills up at noon not only with residents and visitors to the house but with people from the streets and neighbourhood. Guests. There's no telling who might show, but most are a little bent and weather-worn. These are the broken and recovering and limited, Aiden says, the brothers and sisters of addiction, dislocation, exploitation, back-alley politics. Not unlike the two of us, Aiden smiles. All are welcome. No tickets are necessary, no need to phone ahead. There is always a midday meal, a good soup, bread, salad, a sandwich or two. Coffee, tea, a cookie, and fruit, to follow.

Aiden gives me a spot at one of the round tables, pulls out the last chair, pats me on the shoulder, says he'll take care of me, and do I like potato soup?

"Thank you, yes."

Two blue bird women, twins, catch my eye, eating together, across the table. They eat in perfect rhythm, bite for bite, spoon to mouth, like synchronized swimmers. There are seven other tables with four to six chairs around each table; people sitting and enjoying their meal. Sebastian is sitting on a bench against a wall, in conversation with a woman in a well-travelled green trench jacket. There's music on somewhere, coming from the back kitchen, something classical, Bach, those little quick notes, like fireflies. Aiden returns, delivers the soup, sits himself to my right, says a little grace for the two of us, crosses himself, then spoons in.

At my left, another man. He smells of salt. He has a hawk nose and a large peppered beard; loose, matted hair falling over his temples. His large body is arched over the bowl of potato soup, the spoon in his right hand working overtime as he slurps and feasts. Next to him two young men and a young woman eat, students with study books at their side. They discuss course and text. From what I hear they must be taking Sebastian's class. One of the books is the poetry of Meister Eckhart; another is de Chardin's *The Phenomenon of Man*.

After the meal, Aiden inquires if I have any domestic talents, a way in which I might offer myself so that the functioning of the house could benefit from my presence. For now that means two things: hauling the compost materials out back and working them into the three-bin system, and kitchen duty, scrubbing dishes, scouring pots, adding the necessary elbow magic. So into the kitchen I'm escorted, again under the personal shade of Aiden's wing. In the kitchen I'm introduced to a handful of kitchen folk. I'm told by Aiden not to get too hooked on the names. The kitchen is the one place in the house where the names and faces often change. It's strictly volunteer work in the kitchen, people sign up a week or two ahead, plan a meal, collect the materials, come in, make their borscht, chicken broth, cream soup, and salads and sandwiches, whatever is dreamed up. There's order but of a spontaneous nature. Aiden remembers a very fine paella prepared by a Spanish family who happened by the house for a month or so.

"It's an art," he says, "the way things happen here."

The work here is simple. A matter of angelic service, an invisible leavening, the work that radiates from the whole body, instinctual to the heart and hands. The work that matters here is fermenting work, the work of making a grape a wine, making love and life a joy. Sebastian encourages this.

"When we discover not other lands' resources and a means of profit, but a fully conscious joy," Sebastian says, "then the justice we crave will find its course."

In this house, if you happen to work the conventional nine-to-five, or even night work, round-the-clock stuff, you pitch in ten percent of your earnings to help the house meet its needs. There are workers in construction here, there are factory workers, people of the rust-toned infrastructure. There are those who teach and those who have been laid off, cut back, disenfranchised. They come here because the doors are open. If you can't find work out there, then there's the work within the house. Painting the walls, cleaning the can, waxing the hardwood floors, clearing plates, cleaning tabletops, serving soup, cutting bread, pouring water, juice, tea, coffee, wine on special occasions. You offer the experience of your hands, of touch and grace.

Impossible for a world that is round and in orbit to turn away from itself. In this house the tabletop is a place where we gather and share in the yeast of our aliveness.

After helping in the kitchen, Sebastian shows me the meditation room he has recently completed. It's in the back of the house, an old den that has been expanded into a half room, half solarium overlooking the garden and yard. There are eight chairs arranged in a circle. Four more chairs and a few meditation pillows are placed against the back wall. The walls are painted as a soft, blue sky. A small replica of that Russian icon, *The Trinity*, hangs in the centre of the back wall. We sit quietly for twenty minutes. The students join us. Sebastian reads from St. John, "Before Abraham was, I *am*." He reads the line three times, slowly. This strange Christian koan. This lived mystery. I close my eyes and sink into the heart.

I head up to the Danforth on an errand. I walk east along Carlton, through old Cabbagetown, down into the Riverdale basin, cross the footbridge over the Don Valley road and river system, and up to Broadview. It's been a few years since I've walked this neck of the world. On the Danforth I slip into the Carrot Common and pick up the herbs and curry spices I'm after. I have a meal in mind for the house. I walk a different route on the way back, crossing the Bloor-Danforth viaduct. I stop on the bridge. I take in the air of this winter day. It's not too cold. I feel the subway trains rattle beneath my feet. Cars pass at my back, leaving a soft spray of snow and slush. I look south over the Don River with all its mud flats and faded winter grasses, a sprinkling of snow cover. Black river waters push downstream, struggle round floating debris. I look north to edges of the ravine where slivers of my childhood took root. Trees, old and young, heavy branches bare and bent; nothing in bloom along the upper valley hillsides. I look back below to the endless passing traffic, a maze of roads and highways and railway tracks, electrical lines and light standards and the old brick factory, a pit dug into the side of the escarpment. I turn my gaze back south. I can smell the lake in the distance, a hard metallic odour. Smokestacks pump on. I can hear the cutting drone of cars and trucks speeding up and merging, everything coming and going with such speed and clarity that there is little room or time to doubt or question our course.

I close my eyes and breathe it all in, and back out. My pulse slows. My heart hums like fire through damp wood.

As much as I struggled like the river to reconcile myself with the ashes and dignity of loss, there is just now this quiet, elemental felt-sense of deep knowing and remembrance, arising in the wholeness of my breath: I am that emergent being made in the image and likeness of this God-soaked Universe. I am Evolution made flesh. One has to realize reconciliation with one's heart and source and secret-rooms, love reality exactly as it is, or suffer chasing endless lack.

This is it, I think. These are the roads, this is the river, our microcosmic expression. From outer space we're hardly noticeable. Yet it is said of God that not a hair on any head is forgotten. So, we'll sing our songs, we'll light our candles, we'll stomp our feet. Along the way we'll risk ourselves for the lives of those we love. This moment will yield to inevitable bone. Yet even this is soaked in meaning and wine and a faith to say yes.

Enough of the heights and these thoughts without a leg to stand on, I smile. I move west across the viaduct, turn left and go down the steep hillside through the bramble and trees. I wander around the bottomland, hop a few fences, dodge the traffic, trains and tracks, and get as close to the old river flow as humanly possible. I follow the river's southbound curve, let my feet sink and spiral. I spot the odd duck paddling upon the dark waters. I see a band of citizens in big fisherman boots standing along the shoreline, busy hauling out old tires and rusted springs and plastic bags and empty cans, and a refrigerator from the river. I look into the soiled reflection of sky and water, sense things quickening, then slowing and expanding. I walk as far as I can until everything seems to open like a vision into a many-layered intersection of exchange, where the river and the roads come together. For a brief instance I get close enough to people in their cars and behind their dashboard altars so that I can make out the fragrance of all their divine colours. Then the vision tilts and spills off into the dark, churning winter river. I get down on hands and knees and feel across the humpbacked earth for its snow-covered roots. I look up and see the local incinerator, burning signal of grey against the clouds.

This is winter, yes. It will give way to spring. There will be the perennial floods, blossoms, and berries. Summer will undress us with its heat. For some it will be a good year, for others it will be a time to walk an unmapped road. Autumn will take us back down and in; winter will teach us again about silence.

Here we are, immersed in the Universe, this system-of-systems; this love story in the making. I look into the waters and into the deep afternoon skies. I taste the generosity of Creation. I am nothing without these trees, this water, this air, the soil, the sun. After years of wandering and wondering, the clusters of stars and dust and cells and organs that make up my body now know themselves from the inside out. For a moment I see my arms as branches, wild, going out, supporting and being supported, tinged with the curvature of space. Every rippling curve that spirals out of my body does so in response to the embrace of space. I feel this other sap moving through my limbs, deeper shoots, leaves bright with afterbirth.

I move back along the riverside and find those citizens by the river still up to their waists hauling out debris. As I pass a woman calls out, half in jest and half serious, I think, and asks if I want to help out. That is that. I borrow myself a pair of those fisherman hip-hugging rubber boots and nestle into the riverside and start hauling. God is in relationship.

What will become of us? I don't know. Will we make ourselves into the image and likeness of more speed, armour, and monetary gain? Will we shudder as a woman with child, burst out of ourselves as with a big bang, and experience the warm bread of others. Will we do the great groundwork of the caterpillar and butterfly into a poem or a symphony or a scientific breakthrough; will we gather the tragic in our hearts and stand in concert with a matured vista that holds the health and welfare and enhancement of the whole Earth community and all that we are enfolded by to be our primary passion as human beings? I wish I could say. This is what needs my deep care, art, and cultivation, I think. These are the waters, the rivers and lakes, the soils, roots and trees, the streets and people with which I live. Nothing is as I want or will it to be. But this I've come to see; wisdom shows its face along the fault lines of our previous steps. Loving curiosity is the face as we endeavour to take the next. The sacred is like a verb embedded in a thought, and reveals itself in how we imagine what kind of humans we want to be. I will participate in the unfolding, yes. I will fail forward and thrive.

COSMOS

In the world of names, Ana is derived from gift, the giver of self.

She asks to meet in a place where Canada most celebrates its sense of cultural diversity, where its pulse is least felt as a burden or a threat. Where people gather and exchange glances and stories and a philosophy of being. Where the newspapers are free.

The doughnut shop.

We hold hands across a space of less than two feet of tabletop.

"I won't hold you to anything," I say, "not even if you say yes."

Ana.

It's not that we don't want to speak, to fill in the details of the months we've been away from one another, our every step and prayer, the waves of seasons we've travelled. We know deep down all the roads we've entrusted ourselves to, all we have promised ourselves.

"I don't know why I feel so strange when I feel so at home," she says. "Most lovers would be happy just to be back with someone they love."

"Most would be running back to their bedroom," I say.

She slips her hands up under my sleeves.

The walls of the doughnut shop are covered in framed poster prints of Toronto's sports team logos: the Leafs, the Argos, the Blue Jays. There are also framed photo prints of famous Greek sites: the Acropolis, Santorini, Crete.

Across the room, a group of semi-bearded teenage boy-men gather, huddle like wolves, in from last night's prowl. The boy-men are decked out in Michael Jordan sweatshirts and jackets and Chicago Bull hats, and showing off their flashy brand new black-and-red Jordan shoes. The boy-men are busy with hands, slam-dunking doughnut bits over the shoulder, behind the back, over coffee mug rims. Unlit cigarettes propped behind their ears. Their words are slick, untamed, worked, and reworked, lose letters along the way. The two young women sitting with the boy-men remain still, their hands under thighs against swivel seats that are drilled into the floor.

Cosmo, the man who owns and operates this particular doughnut establishment, slips out from behind his counter, moves across the room with a fresh pot of coffee. He has the shoulders of a bull moose, large swaying flanks. His black button shirt hangs open at the chest, revealing a thick, gold crucifix. He moves in on our coffee mugs with all the grace of a thunderstorm.

"How ya doin'?" he asks. "Good time being had?"

"Yes, thank you." We nod.

He refills our mugs, then pulls away.

"Been here a long time," he says to the boy-men and two young women. "No school today or what?"

"No nothin' today," one says, all forehead and chin.

"There's gotta be somethin'," Cosmo says, pouring coffee into their mugs. "When I was your age, well, I was on a boat heading here. Had a wife, a small kid, all I wanted was to be a working stiff. Here I am."

"Here you are, Big Pop." A second boy grins.

"Twenty-four years and counting." Cosmo smiles. "Two wives later, three more kids, four more shops. The Promised Land."

Cosmo squares himself back across the shop and places the coffee pot back on its burner, then turns to the phone on the wall, making a call while refreshing his mouth with a mint breath spray.

One of the boys catches my eyes, rolls his own, then asks if I want a smoke or somethin'.

"Sorry, no," I say, "don't smoke."

"Then why you two looking at us?"

"Sorry again," I say. "We're just talking, catching up."

"Look like you're all ears to me," the boy says. "Look like you got somethin' else on your mind."

"You got me there. You got me fine," I say.

"Thought so." The boy smiles.

"Actually, we're making wedding plans," I say. "Pondering dates, seasons."

"Wedding plans!" the boy says, an unexpected grin taking shape.

"Cool," one of the young women says, turning on her hands to look at Ana. Those eyes.

"Wow," the boy says, sitting up then slumping back. "Don't know how you can be considering marriage in this day and age. It's a crapshoot, a fifty-fifty chance, even less. Look at Cosmo. You gotta be crazy to try something like that."

"I think it's sweet," the young woman says.

"I do too," I say.

"Right," the boy says, grinning. "If you say so."

That said, he stands, clicking his fingers, doing his best Brando. The other boy-men and the young woman stand up right behind him, obedient.

"Where to now?" I ask.

"Wherever the snow won't mess with my shoes," he says, tongue against cheek, spinning away, stepping out.

The morning light fills the store, works across the doughnut counter. New customers appear. Cosmo serves everyone up, a halo grin.

"Oh Canada." Ana smiles.

"I'll take you to Niagara Falls one day." I squeeze her arm.

"You're sure you want to marry me?" She then whispers, "There's so much we don't know about each other."

"There's so much we don't know about a lot of things," I say. "I'm just looking forward to the day we give names to our children."

Her eyes meet mine, her midnight gaze. A light in a single window in a village of twelve homes.

"June has a fresh ring to it," she says, after a while.

Through the years every choice along the road has brought with it a certain terror. The risk of more loss. So that I've second-guessed decisions that might contain light. Until now. Her tender finger moves against my arm under my sleeve. To be saved requires the dignity of touch.

Ana puts this to me: Is there a place in this city where you have yet to reconcile yourself? How she reads me, I don't know. The power of her own grief and journey, intermingling with a desire to know another's heart and land. "We become more complete in the company of other people's sorrows," she says.

We take a walk. The day is cold and bright, clinging to our faces as we angle north toward Bloor and Church, then skirt west to Yonge Street. Traffic at a standstill. We make our way up Yonge to Davenport, turn and wind west past Bay, curving northwest until reaching Avenue Road. As we draw closer, I feel my feet slowing up, overwhelmed by a familiar world. I've been here before. One moves closer to these old haunts, like a visitor to someone else's life, only to find the haunt twisting up from one's own insides.

PILGRIM

I pause at the corner of Avenue Road and Davenport, looking north. I see the dip in the road.

"Here?" Ana says, taking my hand.

"Close," I say.

The street appears much the same. Snow piles line the curb. Just the smell of the wet pavement is enough to take me down. A coarse sensation moves through my body, skeletal images shake. I did not expect to be swallowed whole again by destiny. This place of unyielding descent and disorder of breath. Father, Elle. Nothing has changed and everything has changed.

We cross the street and step north, down into the dip of road and snow, traffic grinding on. I scan the southbound curb side for debris, looking for Father's and Elle's luminous shadows, a stirring again. Residuals of presence.

I stop in my tracks.

We stand over the pothole at the side of the road where I once lay shrouded, my face covered in that wool cardigan, buttonholes in place of my eyes. Bare branches above my head, stutter-tongued. The things I witnessed then; the shadow-events leading to our deaths, the slowing of an orbit, dark matter between our cries. I saw how the power of night eroded the practice of day. Snow on my burning thighs.

Ana's hand moves around my waist, pulling me close.

She takes the blue tissue paper from her pocket, held by her for the months we had been away from one another. I recognize the fold and contents within the tissue.

"What would you like to do with these?"

We attend to the silence of Father's ashes and a prayer for Elle. Bent together near the side of the road, joined in our kneeling, letting the ashes drift and settle. A place of earth that becomes their new skin.

I did not fight my eyes from being touched again by a blue splash of snow and thaw and tears. A gentle flow from an abundant heart.

Sebastian welcomes Ana with a kiss on both cheeks and a warm embrace. He leads us into the kitchen. Aiden and Sebastian's daughter, Tula, join us. Sebastian steps into the pantry and steps back out with a bottle of wine. He uncorks the bottle and sets it on the tabletop, letting the wine breathe. Tula retrieves five glasses. Aiden prepares a board of cheeses and black olive tapenade and slices of French stick and sets the board down on the tabletop. Sebastian looks each of us in the eyes and pours out five glasses of a rich, red Rioja.

"To the temple that is two hearts in love," he says, raising a glass.

Night skies circle in the presence of a new moon.

What is it to lose a life and to find a life? The journeywork of two people navigating the world of oceans and nations, constellations gleaming in their orbits and trysts, only to resurface now like a reed, two lily pads moored nearer the crest of our ample touch.

I stroke the bottom of Ana's left foot, the smooth, worked curve of her sole. How many journeys in the kisses I leave, the oils I work into her skin, the sloping warmth of her thighs.

I focus on her breathing, inhale the widening tone of her heartbeat.

On the windowsill, the candle we've lit hand by hand. Light sheds a lavender scent. Our bodies burn without thirst, nothing manifesting death.

I can see the reflection of my eye in the small pool of oil on her belly. I trace a moistened path down toward the curls of glowing hair round her pubis, buoyant night fruit.

When I kiss her there her whole body shudders.

For this we enter a pilgrimage of desire, unveiling a healing warmth. We bow to the darkness of inner soils, a seed's sacred trust. Our bodies pure blue heat. Her legs are like long-stemmed wildflowers weaving green in a vase. Her breasts brushed with the aroma of descent, the workings of oils and sweat. Her breasts brushed and balanced with the seven days of creation.

Our bodies contain the green prints of who we are, of where we've been, the way fields contain in their folds the designs of water tables, streams in their primal functions, currents of loosened light.

We descend into listening, we descend into our sex. Carrying lineage, carrying the cup of life.

This morning Ana and I spent time organizing Father's paintings in the storage space I had rented a few years ago. There are small, colourful fall sketches of cedar knots, white pine ancestry, bark-peels the rough shape of a canoe. A yellowing birch bending in breeze. There's an unfinished canvas attempting to show the curve of an orange skin in against the small curve of Mother's breasts, sun striking the blonde storm that was her hair. And there's the only self-portrait Father ever painted. His eyes look helpless; his hair sweeping dark and anxious. His mouth questioned death; the lips whose untested scrolls laboured with faith, preening hunger, preening loss. I only interpret the work this way because of the date on the painting, October 1973. Six months after Mother's death. I imagine Father's hands submerged somewhere beneath the canvas's woven flesh, preparing the tracts of ashes and myth, the roads I'll have to walk just to reach this moment.

We return to the house with four paintings. They hang on the north wall of the Welcome Room, celebrating in their own unique journeys of autumn, emergence, and delight.

We bow our heads.

Thank you. *Gracias. Merci.*

Printed in Canada